Michael Britten

This novel is dedicated to the following individuals, without whom, I would be floundering in hyperspace.

Many thanks to my wonderful wife, Vanessa Britten, who made an infinite amount of sacrifices to help me in my quest for publication. Her enthusiasm and love helped me through the dark moments of indecision and self-doubt. I love and respect you.

This novel would not have come to fruition without the friendship, guidance, and technical support of Colin F Barnes. An author extraordinaire, and, I am glad to say, a very good friend. Any mistakes are mine, and mine alone.

CHAPTER ONE

R ed opened her eyes and absently wiped blood from her face. She lay there for a moment, controlling her breathing, assessing, as best she could, where she was. She could see that her body was lying within the tattered remains of a cargo hold.

The floor was hot, as was the air. Fragments of the shattered hull littered the floor. Above her, an unforgiving sun radiated down through splinters of broken panels. Escaping gasses made her turn her head. A guidance system lay dormant, and above it, several fractured pipes billowed-out white swirls of hot mist. With a grating rattle, the carcass of the ship finally exhaled and died.

Red looked down her body and inspected her G-suit for tears, or foreign objects – everything seemed in order. She searched her mind for any recollection of the flight, but remembered nothing.

A desk panel reflected her image. She gazed at her face, those dark eyes, reflective, innocent – but unrecognisable. The image, a stranger to her, made her feel uncomfortable.

She saw smears of blood. Red put a hand to her face and started searching for wounds, but found none. Only one logical explanation came to mind. The blood belonged to someone else. Five thick red smears streaked down towards her chin. She looked at the marks again in the reflection and now saw that a hand must have caressed her face.

Red got to her feet. Before she made the fatal error of stumbling blindly forward, she breathed deeply and fought to regain a sense of calm.

"There is nothing to fear. You are not in danger," she said aloud and recoiled — she did not recognise her own voice.

Why was her memory defying her? First her image, and now her voice was alien. She shook her head in frustration and looked at the Guidance system area. The escaping gasses were hydraulic compounds. Beneath the ship lay energy tanks, both of which had surely fractured. Together, these compounds were a deadly concoction. Inhaled, they could induce a temporary amnesia.

Red put a hand to her mouth. How did she know this information? Was she a science officer, or maybe a shuttle tech? Next to where she had awoken lay a life pod. A splintered canopy exposed an empty interior. More crimson smears stained the soft cream fabric. Red turned the puzzle over in her mind. Someone – someone injured – had most likely opened her capsule to remove her body. A new thought took her, that she might not be alone. Red scanned her surroundings, checking every corner and shadow, but nobody was there.

The deck on which she stood ran on and met with the hot golden sand, which stretched out and vanished into the shimmering horizon. The ship's cockpit lay some distance away, steaming and dead. As she surveyed the wreckage, she noticed more debris lying some way off. Something did not look right.

Red raced along the deck and then her flight boots slapped against the soft sand of the desert, towards a large, trough-like indent. The area looked churned; the patterns were erratic, as if a group of individuals had circled what must have been another pod.

Drag-marks stretched away. Red followed the line with her eyes. The markings travelled up the dune and continued over the summit.

Red sprinted forward, her legs pumping hard as she climbed, her eyes scanning the soft contours of the dune as she rose higher. Maybe she still had time to save her crewmember. At the very least, she might get to see the captors as they heaved away their cargo. Her boots travelled the same path, sometimes digging into the same indentations as the previous climbers.

She reached the top and stopped. The dune fell away again, and the tracks continued down before stopping abruptly. New markings, large and deep, hinted at some kind of vehicle. The pod and the footprints vanished, and the new patterns stretched into the distance... to an impossibly large construction.

A vast city wall ran to her left and right before vanishing in the heat. The walled medina looked ancient and incredible against the barren background.

Must be one of the sand cities, Red thought to herself. Again, she flinched at the memory recall. The phrase, sand city, had come to her mind quickly, but the structure did not look familiar, and she did not know its name. She took a deep, hot breath.

Remembering the crash, Red looked over her shoulder. From her vantage point, she saw the impact markings and all the debris. She scanned the scene. Life-pods, her mind said. Why were they in life-pods? Was their journey really that far to need stasis? She brushed the question aside.

A person, most likely injured in the crash, pulled her free from her broken capsule. She resisted the urge to contemplate who this person was and concentrated on what she knew as fact. The dark recesses of her mind told her she had been in a type 2 shuttle. She found no markings standing out amongst the debris field, which went against all codes of travel. Her suit did not have any insignias, either. Even the helmets within the craft had no corporate identities.

She scanned the land. The desert stretched in all directions, harsh, forbidding and impossible to cross without sufficient equipment. She turned and looked again at the vast walled medina. Logic dictated her course of action – her only course of action, she told herself. The city would either reunite her with the other crewmember, or be her downfall. Red took a deep breath and started down the dune.

Chapter Two

Energy conservation and hydration were Red's top priority. She used her time well, stimulating her mind with mental exercises. Yet despite her efforts, picturing the ship's consoles and imagining herself going about her duties did nothing to induce a response.

The city loomed nearer, and she marvelled at its enormity. A soft wind blew, scattering the tracks before her until they were barely visible.

The tracks led to iron sheet doors that rose to nearly the full height of the wall. Even from a distance, the surface rust showed the harshness of this hostile land.

Red looked up, inspecting the top of the wall. She saw no guards or watchtowers. Covering the last few yards of open sand, Red reached the doors and stopped.

On her left-hand side, at head height, was a comm panel with a hand-scanner, which was a good way of the city getting access to a visitor's fingerprint, or DNA.

Tentatively, she touched the metal. Then she placed a hand on the hot plate. Static suddenly crackled and then a barrage of single words erupted until a word in her own language that simply said, "Speak."

"I'm a survivor of a downed craft and I need your help," she said, trying to be as succinct as possible.

The voice, again in her own language, said, "Welcome."

Red imagined a barrage of further instructions, but a loud popping sound announced that the micro-conversation was over. She waited.

A sound like gas expelling made her step back. The enormous doors juddered as whatever mechanism came into play. Slowly, the sheets of metal parted.

The doors continued along their track, sending up a large plume of dust. Red waved the air until it cleared, and then she had her first glimpse of the city beyond.

A riot of sounds and smells greeted her, awakening her senses. Crowds of people swarmed erratically. A man with dusty orange skin pushed a sleeve back and beckoned her to approach through a sandstone arch that stood a few feet beyond the main doors.

Red stepped forward and passed through the object. As her body entered the sandy device, she saw tiny lights, pin-sharp and pulsing. Lasers scanned her form as she passed through the arch.

"Thank you for permitting me to enter," she said, trying to forge a quick relationship. The man, who didn't seem to understand her, motioned to her again, and pointed at another device.

"Can I speak with someone in charge?" she asked, slowing her speech, but the man merely grinned at her through what remained of his front teeth, and continued to point at the machine. He even pulled at her shoulder with one bony hand, encouraging her to move forward.

Red approached the block and looked at the worn panel. Crude pictorial carvings told her what she must do. A hole was in the sandstone, just wide enough to insert a hand. She turned around to look at the dark skinned man. He grinned and nodded his head. Red turned back to the machine, drew in a breath and did as asked.

Something quickly grabbed her, and she gasped. Red yanked her arm back. There, around her wrist, was a metal bracelet, thick, with yet more bleeping speckles of light.

She turned to the gate-man to express her dissatisfaction, but he had gone back inside what was surely his sentry-post. A small rivet encrusted door slid down, shutting him off.

Red inspected the bracelet. It was light, and as she turned it, she could find not one connection, as if they fashioned it from a single piece of metal.

This was not a good start. She looked back at the entrance and debated leaving, but decided that heading off into the desert without sufficient equipment would be foolish.

Exploring the city seemed to be her best option. She comforted herself with the notion that she might find her shipmate.

After the silence of the dunes, the noises of the medina sounded harsh and aggressive. Everyone seemed to shout at once. The swell of the crowd moved like an angry sea as she made her way in and around tired, bleached market stalls.

She marvelled at the diversity of life that mingled together. Desert trekkers covered in many layers of cloth rubbed shoulders with dark skinned warriors who carried their wares on tall sticks or suspended from their belts by ropes. Three women walked towards her wearing black clothing. Their white painted faces and shaven heads gave them a serene radiance. Crude drawings of flames adorned their porcelain-smooth foreheads. One of them suddenly looked at Red, her black outlined eyes wide and piercing. Red tried not to stare, but found it impossible. The sight of these rather attractive women was strangely hypnotic.

The market seemed to stretch on forever. She passed fire pits where strange looking animals were roasting on spits. A gathering stood near, devouring crispy flesh, their fingers slimy and their teeth dark and crusted. Red moved past them, feeling a little queasy as she breathed in the charcoal fumes.

She stopped and gasped when someone riding a creature cut through the crowd and headed her way. Red moved aside, making way for the lumbering animal. It had a wide, brownish body and a short, thin neck that supported the tiniest of heads. From its mouth ran two leather straps, which its owner held in his pudgy hand. The large man wore fine looking clothes of pale blue and gold. His wealth was clear. His oily looking chest, with its bristling carpet of hair and heavy folds of skin, lay bare for all to see. Trinkets hung about the man's round neck and chubby wrists. As he passed, he seemed to consider Red, standing still amongst the bustle, but the man did not stop his passage. He looked down at her with contempt, as if she were something from the gutter. Red stayed to watch the animal with its repugnant cargo go sailing past.

She let out a sigh as she looked about. This was going to be difficult, she told herself. Far too many people filled this city, and the thought of finding her crewmember seemed slim. If she had no luck finding her friend... Red stopped and considered the word for a moment. Just how well did she know this person? Nothing presented itself, and she let the thought hang. The next thing to do was try bargaining safe passage out of this sector. At least, with this vast array of people, her appearance, with her off-white G-suit, looked unremarkable.

Red looked about and could no longer see the vast walls of the city, such was the variety and density of the surrounding structures. Over the way stood a higher structure — some kind of tower. She put a hand up and covered her eyes as she considered the building. A glint of light came and went. She spied people up there. Were they watching the crowds, she wondered? Fanning her face for a moment, she stood wondering which way to go. Her senses were tingling from the rich environment. All of this was so alien to her... or was it, she wondered?

Before she could take another step, someone pulled Red from the crowd. The grip was tight and the tug no accident.

"What are you doing?" she protested, twisting her body to see who, or what, was pulling at her.

A face came menacingly close to her own. It was a man. A round ruddy face peered out from beneath a frame of white dusty head cloth. He had an enormous nose and an even wider mouth. Two insipid eyes considered her.

"Follow me if you want to live," he said in a broken accent.

The man continued to pull Red off to his left. He did not seem to care how rough he was being as he pulled her between two stalls. When they were standing out of sight between the billowing canopies, he pulled her closer and turned her about, his mighty hands moving her with ease. His heavy chest pressed against her back and his arm went around her neck. Then his beefy hand cupped her mouth. His palm was oily and she could smell sweat and spices.

Red tried to break free, but with every twist and objection, she felt the immense man tighten his hold upon her. Her body was still sluggish from the crash and the person's strength greater than her own. She saw people passing, but they could not see her. With no way of overturning the situation, Red stilled her body and waited. If the person had wanted her dead, it would have already happened. Breathing deeply, she waited to find out why she was being held.

Chapter Three

Manark breathed in and untied his top button. His eyes considered the message on his data screen. The words Syrin sat there, like the name of an old jilted lover. He swallowed as he opened it. The contents did not help to ease his concerns. He thought, after so many years, that the piece of work he had done on the Arin project for the corporation was closed for good. He reread the message.

Why summon for him now, he wondered? It had been what? Five years. He had been confident about the service he had provided. He closed the pad and sat back in his chair and thought. The Arin project. It had been a while since he had thought about that name. The time on his wall illumination counted out the seconds. The invite was clear. It gave him two days to comply. Two days? He wouldn't last two hours, thinking about why they had asked for him.

He remembered how spritely he had walked into their lobby on his first day. And the work had been rewarding enough. But there was something not right about the company — something dark that whispered to his inner instinct. He had finished his work and got out of there. No, that wasn't exactly true. He had worked up to a certain point and then... and then a firm hand-shake and a final pay. The smile and the positive critique of his work file should have put a smile on his face. But again, he sensed unsaid things.

Turning his data pad back on, he vid-dialled Syrin. The meeting would happen immediately. He had to know what they wanted. Shaking his head, he reminded himself that he had done nothing wrong, that he had fulfilled every aim that they had set. And yet, why did he feel like he was being called in to be reprimanded? Lifting his finger, he clicked on the link and waited. A blue pulse flashed in the corner of his screen to show a dialling connection. He looked at the link in the bottom left corner and realised that this was not the appointment secretary. He read the name and felt his hands tremble. This was a direct line to Sarak.

· · · ● · ● ● · · ·

Red battled to break free, but the large man hugged her closer. He leaned his head to her ear and whispered, telling her to watch. His hand that cupped her mouth moved her head a little to the left.

Red saw, through the gap in the trade stalls, how the crowd suddenly dispersed. Then, lines of men wearing dark grey uniforms marched past. Leather caps with dark visors obliterated their faces; they carried sharp-tipped staffs point up, like banners as each person swung their arms in time with the next.

These soldiers passed by, eight, ten, fifteen - it was hard to tell exactly how many came and went. Then the last one appeared wearing a white uniform. The man paused beside a stall. Red watched as the soldier grabbed hold of the trader there, pulling him by his collar. He said something to this dishevelled man. The trader looked terrified and shook his head, negatively. The soldier, displeased with the response, shoved the man to the floor before continuing on his way.

Red felt the big man behind her relax. She twisted herself free of his grip.

"What is the meaning of his?" she said, panting hard and rubbing at her wrist with her hand.

"They are looking for you," he said, his voice still a whisper.

"That can't be," she said. "I've only just arrived; besides, they don't know me."

The man before her pointed at her wrist. "They have tagged you on entry. We need to get that removed, quickly."

Red looked at the band about her wrist. Then she noted the one on the man's wrist.

"But you have a band, as well."

"It is the law here," he said. Then he smiled. "But it hasn't stopped me getting the information doctored." He pointed a finger at her. "In addition, my new friend, they are not looking for me. They are looking for you."

"But what could they want with me?" she asked.

The man stroked his sweating palms down his enormous chest and breathed in. "I know. Let's stay here until they find us and you can ask them, right before they take you below ground for interrogation. Alternatively, I can take you somewhere to have that bracelet removed. The choice is yours."

Red considered the man's words. She pictured the way the uniformed person had tossed the stallholder aside, and she knew exactly how an interrogation would go.

"I haven't been here for long, but already, I'm not impressed. People harassed, strangers grabbing hold of me..."

"I don't blame you," the big man said. "It is a harsh place. If I were a more disciplined man, I would leave this hole and find a better home." He gestured about with his hands. "Three hundred years ago we colonised this planet and look what we have. I wish my ancestors had stayed on earth."

Red considered him and shook her head. "If I'm being honest, I don't know if I can trust you," she said, her body still poised, ready to turn and run.

The man shrugged his shoulders. "I will not stand here persuading you. If you do not want my help, then take your chance outside. Once they find out you're hiding, they will call in for an area scan and that will be the end of the matter."

"Why don't they just scan for me now, if they want to find me?"

The large man shook his head. "Your bracelet is new – the information is probably being processed as we speak. But imputing is not instant." He glanced at the Digi-clocks hanging from a stall. "Soon you will be logged, so time is of the essence. We don't have fancy tech like in the cities. A file has to be made, and then coded."

"Why do you want to help me?"

The man suddenly put out his hand, making Red flinch. "Come with me and I'll tell you as we go. If you don't like what you hear, then you can shout for help."

Red looked at his sizable hand and then across at the streaming sunlight. Her intuition told her to continue on her way, but then she pictured her crewmember, who was somewhere out there. She sighed and reluctantly took the man's hand.

His grip was tight. He turned and forced his way in and around the back of the stalls. He clambered over discarded boxes and slipped once or twice on rotting discarded produce. Red smiled each time he cursed. Her balance was much better, being slight.

Red waved her free hand across her nose as the stench of waste met her nostrils. The big man then led them down narrow alleyways with old, blistered doorways and rough stone baked sand-bricks, and the stench faded. Red followed behind, her eyes scanning the surroundings.

"Tell me your name?"

The man glanced back over his shoulder. "It's Jar."

"Jar...? I can't call you Jar," Red said, frowning, despite him not being able to see. Then the man stopped and turned.

"My name is Roofinilusjar. Can you say that?"

Red looked at him. "Jar it is."

"Good. Now we are getting somewhere."

Jar, who seemed content with the outcome, turned and started forward with Red in tow.

"So why are you helping me?"

"Those bastards took my daughter," he said without turning around. "Those men accused her - they do this all the time."

"They took her where?"

"Under the city is a vast area of tunnels. That is where they operate. People call them Janicans, which in our language means sand moles. There is a decider room, and that is where they took her."

"Why haven't they released her?" Red asked.

Jar stopped and turned, wiped his forehead, then fanned his face with the palm of his hand.

"Lots of people get taken down there, but few return. So who knows? She was young, like you, and beautiful."

"Why haven't you protested?" Red asked, studying his face.

"This is a sand city. They do things differently here. I have waited many months. It is hard to get anything from them. I have my ways. A contact has told me she is dead."

Red studied his face more intently. He kept his eyes neutral and unblinking.

"But there are many ways to make someone pay for this," he said. "It came to my attention, most recently, who gave the order to kill her. I have been biding my time. I will make him pay. Helping you escape them is like a small... how do you say? Hit on the wrist."

"Slap on the wrist," Red corrected. "Okay. I believe you. Now where are you taking me?"

"I don't have to take you anywhere," he said. "We are already here."

Jar turned and tapped on a door. He waited and then tapped three times, spacing out each rap. Evidently, this was a code, because within seconds Red heard bolts sliding.

"Do not worry," Jar said. "This place has a blocking facility. You will soon lose that contraption."

The narrow door revealed a dark room. Jar walked in first, dipping his head to pass through.

Red stood a moment longer, assessing the situation.

Jar, realising that she was not following, turned.

"You will be safe in here," he said.

Sensing the importance of time, Red looked back down the narrow walkway, back to the billowing canvases and the distant noise of the market. It was one thing to run away down streets she didn't know, but to enter a dark, unfamiliar building with a stranger was a different level of risk.

"Once you go live on their system, they can scan and they will have you," he said.

Red looked back at him before she delicately stepped into the dwelling and let the gloom claim her.

Chapter Four

T he coolness of the room was a welcomed respite from the harsh sun. Red, however, had little time to bask in this fresh sensation as a sudden shifting sound had her turning.

A person looking neither male nor female moved forward, almost pushing Red out of the way. The person locked the door and scuttled off into the centre of the sizable room.

"This is Gliss," Jar said, indicating the person with an outstretched hand. "He is an electronic artist. Possibly the best in these lands."

"Is that why he operates from this such a dank back street?" Red said.

Jar studied her for a moment before replying.

"Gliss is what the overlords have labelled unworthy."

"An unworthy?"

"It is someone of a low family. They will never permit him to serve in the community - at least not officially, so he has to eke out a living as he can."

"Who are *they*?"

"The overlords."

"They rule here?"

"They think they do," Jar smirked, looking at the old man. "Oh, they try to keep us down but we are cunning."

Red shook her head. "I must say that I don't like the sound of these overlords."

Jar simply nodded and turned to watch Gliss work.

Red looked at the scrawny man with shocking white hair and saw him in a different light. "Do these... overlords know he operates from here?"

"Oh, they know much. However, he is nothing to them... no threat. They let him earn his small credits."

"So there is a rank operation here," she said, but Jar was already shaking his head.

"You ask a lot of questions. That bracelet still needs to come off."

"Wait," Red said as the old man came forward. "I need some information first, before this is removed."

She noted Jar's impatience and an inner voice told her that all was not as it appeared.

"Have you seen another person...? Possibly a female, probably wearing similar clothing to mine."

"No," Jar said, shaking his head. "You are the first today. If your friend arrived here, then they did not come through the same door."

Red nodded her head, feeling frustrated that they had not spotted her crewmember.

"They have a relaxed policy to who they give entry," she said, examining the bangle on her wrist.

"You were lucky," Jar said. "This is a phase. The sun is due to have..." he fought to find the words. "Brief explosions."

"You mean sun-flares?" she said.

"That is it. The flares are terrible. During this phase, they permit anyone entry to Solar 3. When the flare happens, there will be nobody on these streets."

"Solar 3? That's the name of this city?"

"Yes. There are four other outposts. Solar 1 is the biggest, so they say."

"You haven't been there?"

"It is too far through the desert. I have seen Solar 4. It is a short trek. I've been there on... business."

Red nodded her head, taking in the information, and then noticed that the thin man with the straggly hair had vanished.

"You friend hasn't spoken a word," she said.

"He does not understand Majarri speak. He only talks Poocka, and a little Janna."

The word Poocka had a familiarity about it, as if Red had heard it before.

"Come now," Jar said. "Our friend is ready for you in the other room."

Red followed Jar over to a long curtain. He pulled the material back to reveal a wide arch.

Jar looked at her to see her reaction. Before them, standing like a brooding monster, was an impressive looking machine. It had three sections; large round casing, roaming pipework, and an array of pulsing panels. The whole machine, which seemed to have various applications, funnelled down into one small operating area.

The thin man pulled a trolley stool across and motioned for Red to sit.

"Salbon, Salbon," the man said.

"Dalask," Red replied as she went to take a seat. Then she recoiled in surprise.

"You speak Poocka?" Jar said, and then looked at his friend, who looked just as mystified.

Red sat down and thought. How did she know how to reply – and just how much of this language could she speak?

"You look surprised," Jar said. Red saw something in his narrowing eyes that she did not like.

The old man came around to her side, took her wrist, and lifted it. He pulled out a padded plate on a long metal limb and rested her arm there. Turning the head-device twice brought two further implements into play. He chose the smaller of the two.

"Are you sure this is safe?" Red said, glancing at Jar.

"Absolutely so," he said. "He has done many. He can reprogram them for people, giving them some access mostly denied, or he can remove. Removal he doesn't do often," Jar said, holding up his own wrist. "It's the law."

"But won't I need one?" she said, frowning.

"That depends, my friend. Are you planning on staying here?" he said.

Red gave a sigh. "No, I guess not. After I find my friend, I'll be leaving."

"Then it will not matter if we remove it," Jar said.

Gliss moved from Red's side and went to an info panel to start the machine. After a moment, with nothing happening, the tiny man hit a panel. Then he pressed more buttons before hitting the machine once more.

"Are you sure he knows how to operate this?" Red said, still looking along the machine to watch the man.

"Yes, he knows exactly what to do, but this machine is old —" Jar did not get to finish his sentence, however, as Red got up from her seat and walked along to where the old man was standing.

Gliss was gripping a green tube, which he was trying to push downward. He was cursing and willing the pipe to move. Red marvelled at how she could understand what he was saying.

"Chrish dallah," she suddenly said, shoving him out of the way with her elbow. Instead of pushing the pipe back into play, she reached up, threw open a panel and pumped a leaver.

"You haven't primed the tube," she said before catching hold of herself. Again, she swapped looks with the two men, who stared at her in disbelief. Red took a step back and searched her mind for how she knew this machine, but found no answer. Jar suddenly broke into a deep laugh, making Red turn.

"My friend, you are full of surprises," he said. "It is you that is the artist, I see that now."

Red was still reeling. Maybe she was a shuttle tech after all, she thought. Gliss motioned her back to the seat – maybe the physical connection gave her the operating knowledge.

She placed her arm back and the thin man leaned over. Gliss slid the tool onto the surface of the bracelet. Then he returned to the panel.

Red did not want to look, but her head wanted to see what was happening. The bracelet was a tight fit against her wrist.

Various sounds emitted from the machine and the nozzle pulsed with energy.

Red searched her mind to recall what the machine was now doing, but her memory was empty again. The nozzle turned white and then the bracelet itself seemed to come to life. Tiny inscriptions appeared and the bracelet simply clicked open.

So that was it, she thought. The only thing that needed breaking was a code.

"So there we are," Jar said as Red lifted her arm from the plate and rubbed at her free wrist.

"Wow, that's amazing," she said, smiling at the tiny man. Then she saw Jar suddenly go to a dark plate on the far wall.

"What is it?" Red said.

"Sentinel guards," he said, peering through a tiny viewing screen. "Come see."

Red felt a wave of fear run down her spine. She imagined the guards walking right up to their door and knocking, or worse, breaking the door down. She felt certain that these guards would then take her deep underground to be interrogated. She would lose the chance of finding her crew mate, and finding the missing pieces to her memory loss. She had to know if these guards were here for her. Red walked up behind him and Jar turned to her. As he turned, he placed something icy on her neck, making her gasp.

"I am sorry, my friend," he said.

A numbness spread quickly throughout her body. She just had time to glance over at the scrawny man, who was smiling and nodding his head. The room disappeared from her vision as Jar's beefy hands grabbed hold of her shoulders. The last thing she saw of Jar was his eyes. They were humourless and cold, like that of an animal before its prey. Then she had a sinking feeling and darkness claimed her.

Chapter Five

R ed had fleeting moments of recognizing sights and sounds between stretches of oblivion. Jar's rich voice drifted in and out, and then she felt a soft cloth about her head. But then, a moment later, she felt herself being bumped around and squeezed into a box-like container. At least two sets of hands adjusted her arms and legs to fit into the container. A rocking motion stirred her a moment later, and then she detected the sudden hotness of the outside world. This sudden containment triggered older, fragmented memories. She had been held before — the feeling of being trapped in a container flashed through her mind and then faded back into her subconscious.

Without warning, her mind released a name... no, two names. The word White entered her head, and she knew it was a name and not a colour, just as she knew her own name was Red. Another name appeared, also a colour. Blue.

Red awoke to an inner coolness. She opened her eyes and slowly looked around. Fatigue clung to her like a cloak.

About her lay a wide, yet cylindrical, room. She looked up. The ceiling was a fine white dome, calming and carefully decorated in yellow and pink.

Raising a hand, she rubbed her face. The fatigue subsided a little, and she lifted her head.

She was alone and lying on a slightly raised platform, which was circular, to match the contours of the room. A soft material cradled her body - cool to the touch, despite the glorious sunlight that filtered in through the windows in long, translucent shafts of gold.

Her mouth was incredibly dry and her tongue slightly swollen. She spied two dishes lying beside her. One had liquid and the other, some kind of cubed food.

Raising herself, she grabbed at the first dish and sniffed. It had no smell. She put one finger into the liquid and tentatively touched her tongue. The liquid had no taste. She took a chance and drank slowly, willing herself not to consume too much. Satisfied, she went to the other dish and picked up one of the soft chunks. She did not recognise what it was, but it resembled cut fruit. As she ate, she looked about.

The wide room was sparse, with just the bed that she rested upon and, against the wall, a data desk that looked unused. The room had just two windows, one behind her and one in front.

Red stood up on heavy legs and noted her bare feet. A loose-fitting cloth, which fastened by a simple chord belt, had taken the place of her G-suit. The thought of someone undressing her to change her clothing made her feel uncomfortable. Red crossed her arms across her chest, conscious of her nakedness beneath the light fabric.

Massaging her legs to get them moving, Red walked over to one of the slim windows. She looked out. Vast trees obliterated the skyline, blocking the view beyond. Thick vines wormed up the trunk of the nearest tree, which was about six feet away. A fat looking animal sat on the limb. It blinked twice with its tiny eyes before scurrying off.

The view told her nothing, so she walked to the other window. Her legs were quickly regaining their strength, and her head grew less fuzzy. Red reached the window and her heart sank.

She looked at the sprawling city wall, and even the tips of market tents that lay beyond. She could not see down from this window, but deduced that this building was incredibly tall. Given the circular shape of her room, she decided that this was a tower... and the tower was on the outside of the city.

A thought took her, and she turned, her eyes searching. She found no door. Then, as she continued to look, she noticed a dusty looking hatch, which was nearly the same colour as the sandstone. She went over to it and tried to prize it with her fingers, but the trapdoor lay flush and offered no grip. Red searched for a tool of any kind, but found nothing. Then her eyes returned to the dusty data comm.

She moved towards it with a renewed hope. Her hand traced the cool black contours, searching for a button. Still nothing. She inspected further and realised it was hand-scan activated. She placed her hand there, hoping that it was not DNA coded.

A sudden noise had Red turning. Somewhere in the room, a latch operated.

Red retreated to the raised bed area. With the room empty of anything but the bowls beside the bed, all she could do was watch as a face appeared.

Various images filtered through her mind. She pictured Jar's face, and other ogre-like faces, but she never imagined the delicate face of a woman.

The person did not say a word as she entered the room. Apart from her initial glance to see where Red was, the woman acted as if she were alone. She was dark skinned, with thick, unruly shoulder-length hair. She wore a similar dress, but hers was dirty and tattered. Her face, which must have once looked beautiful, was weather-beaten and lined.

Red did not say a word as the woman came to the bed and bent down to pick up the two empty dishes. Red noted hers hard, worn, leather-like palms. This person was no captor – she was a slave.

With her task completed, the servant turned and started back towards the open hatch. Red, so fascinated she had not contemplated escape, but she had to dismiss the thought immediately. When the woman reached the hatch, Red noticed a slight distortion, which vanished when she walked forward. The servant must have had about her person, some kind of sensor that temporarily disarmed the force field. Red realised she was about to leave without as much as a single word.

"Wait."

The woman stopped and looked at her.

"Tell me why I'm being held here," Red demanded.

The woman just stared at her with wild looking eyes.

"Just tell me anything you can?" Red further pleaded, but the woman had already averted her gaze and was carefully descending, pulling the hatch closed behind her.

Red sighed, not believing the predicament. She fought back her emotions. Maybe this woman did not speak Majarri. She knew Poocka. Maybe she could try that language next time the servant appeared.

Red thought about Jar. No wonder he had been so diligent and intent upon ridding her of the bracelet. With no traceable identity, kidnaping was easy. Was this *his* tower, she wondered? She thought not. He was not poor, but he looked more like a trader than a man of wealth. No, her captor, or captors, had yet to reveal themselves.

Another sigh escaped her lips. This place, she decided, was meant to be her cell for some time. Why feed her if her imprisonment was only temporary? Her captor could easily starve her if he intended to trade her – then she would be somebody else's problem. She looked about and decided that this building was old. Why carry her unconscious body to the top of this tower unless it had no service device or lift? Then she considered the bed again and her body tensed. Something told her she was not a typical slave. Her captive could have housed her anywhere for that. No, this room only had one function – she believed her imprisonment was for sexual purposes.

Red wound her arms around herself. Options were still forming in her mind when she heard distant movements. Someone was whistling. The sound drifted up, and the whistle got louder. This musical sound was so carefree that surely it must be her captor. She held her breath, moved back towards the window, and felt the ledge press into her back. Then the hatch opened.

Chapter Six

R ed watched as a bald man ambled up through the hatch. Once out, he straightened.

The man looked as rich as Jar looked ordinary. His fine cloth was a vibrant yellow. His cuffs had a silver thread in tiny, delicate patterns. He was a tall, but portly man. His pale complexion told Red that here was a person who did little physical work; at least, he did not work in the open air. His round face beamed at her. His eyes, unremarkable, sat floating above thick black eyeliner. On his forehead was a large polished stone that shimmered a deep obsidian. How this item fixed to his forehead, she did not know.

"Good, you are awake," he said in her own tongue. His enunciation was precise – delicate, even. "You are strong. It usually takes longer to come round."

Without realising, he had given her information. She was not the first, and probably would not be the last. Red remained silent to keep him talking.

"I trust you are suitably comfortable," he said, gazing around the room as if considering the surroundings for the first time. "It is not a bad room. You have magnificent views - quite remarkable views, actually. Many people would give good money to stay in a room like this."

He paused for a moment and scrutinised her. His small, taut mouth was ugly, Red decided. His stomach was enormous and protruding, a symbol of his wealth and standing. From what she could see, two long, spindly legs supported his upper frame. She looked back at his gut. If she were going to strike, it would be there. A full gut was delicate.

"Very well. I see that you're taking the silent approach. That is all very well. I haven't paid for your conversation."

"Just my sex," Red responded, making sure her voice was calm and clear.

He breathed in, his enormous belly moving his yellow cloth, his face unflinching.

"Yes, that is why you are here, my little bird."

"Was it Jar who sold me?"

"Does it matter?" he said, holding his palm out in mock surrender.

"It matters to me. It matters that I know who put me in this situation."

"You say this situation... it's not as bad as you think. You will get used to this. After a while, you may even gain your own room, overlooking the garden. There's a secure area so that you may walk and take in the air."

"But to have that, I will have to get used to having your enormous belly pressed against me every night."

The man studied her, his face a mask of control, but his eyes let him down – when he spoke again, his voice was like silk.

"Not every night, little bird," he said, his small tight mouth attempting a smirk. "Don't over estimate your importance - there are others."

Red thought about this. She was seeing the bigger picture now. There was more to this dwelling than just a tower. She could not see how large the building was, but there must be many rooms... and other girls, she told herself.

"I want you to spend your time thinking about your situation," he said, his gaze sweeping the room, absently. "This place is secure. Escape is not possible. Calling will not help. These walls are far too thick for sound to escape. There is only one thing that can change. I can stop your food. You will grow weaker and weaker until you won't be able to lift a single arm in protest."

He left his words hanging in the air like a dagger. She saw in his eyes and heard on his tongue how he revelled in his control of the situation – *her* situation. She wondered if he had taken this course before and decided that he had. His tone was one of gloat and yes, she thought, it brought him pleasure.

"So I am to be your pleasure slave?" Red said.

"Ooh, I like that," he replied. "You are going to be good once I've trained you."

"Your arrogance will be your down fall," she said, and saw a little of his sparkle vanish.

"I'm tired of you now," he announced with a wave of a hand. "We have got off to a good start though - you have to trust me on that. I will chat with you soon."

As if showing his control of the situation, he turned his back on her as he retraced his steps to the hatch. Red watched him go. Despite his size, he seemed agile, and he placed his feet carefully as he exited down through the hole. Then the hatch closed, leaving Red alone with her thoughts.

Red exhaled and unclenched her palms. The temptation to attack him had been strong, especially when he had turned his back. She was pleased with her control. She needed him to believe that she would not strike. No, she would let him come to her and go without complication. He was trying to manipulate her. He would have raped her on the first meeting if he had wanted. His arrogance and his sexual preference said that he got a thrill out of converting. This was good. It gave her time, and it meant she could delude him into thinking that she was complying. If she bided her time, he might let down his guard.

Red asked herself a question. Was she capable of violence? Was she a fighter? Most people considered themselves capable, but the reality was far different. She knew she was a thinker, but would she be able to overcome him physically?

She remembered the other visitor. The woman was clearly some kind of servant. Maybe she had once been sitting in this very spot, asking herself the same questions, but she had grown old and he had found other uses for her. Red wondered if this was a weak link. If she could work on this servant, then maybe the hatch might remain open.

As if by thought transference, the hatch opened and the woman in question climbed up the steps, carrying a jug.

The servant looked at her before averting her gaze. Once out of the trap door area, she ambled over and set her jug down on the floor next to the window. For the first time, the woman turned and addressed her directly.

"Daddlity," she said. "Daddlity," she repeated, pointing down at the jug with her dry, withered hand. When Red did not respond, she looked around, searching for an alternative way to communicate.

"What are you trying to say?" Red said, hoping that hearing pure Majarri might show what dialect to use.

The woman came forward, waving her hands. She stood over the jug, placing her feet on either side of the object and half lowering her bony body. Then her hands moved down to her groin and her fingers splayed outwards. She made a gushing sound with her mouth.

"Are you are telling me it's for toileting," Red said, and then wrinkled her nose, which made the woman smile and nod her head.

Red felt sorry for her. Several of her teeth were missing – her lips looked dry. It was a shame, because beneath this person's age and neglect was an incredibly beautiful face.

"Daddlity," Red said, and the woman nodded enthusiastically. She thought about the word and its meaning. Unfortunately, she did not understand this language. Then Red remembered she spoke Poocka. "Jallan Kamah," Red said.

The woman stopped nodding and stared. "Jallan Kamah," Red said again, but the woman shrugged her shoulders. Red shook her head.

"What are we to do, you and me," Red said, going to the woman and placing her hands upon the woman's shoulders. The woman suddenly flinched and backed away, as if stung. She backed further, skirting the perimeter of the room until she reached the hatch. Her scared eyes never left Red as she scurried off down the steps, pulling shut the door behind her.

Red cursed under her breath. She was doing so well and they were forming their first small bond. She had moved too soon. Maybe physical touch had become alien to this woman - or touch reminded her of the bald man with his eager, feverish hands. Maybe this had been the first touch of friendship that this person had ever had.

With little else to do, she squatted down on her bed and rested her head in her hands. She glanced at her new toilet facility and realised she now had a weapon. Red would have to begin again with the servant – the big man, however, whom she had named Mr Jewel, was going to be a challenge. Red hoped the slave would return soon. The word that the woman had used came to mind. As soon as she repeated it, something stirred. Red sat up straight, her breathing increasing, and her eyes unseeing. Something was activating deep within her, working and forming until she could sense nothing else.

Chapter Seven

T he Suite on the eightieth floor was unknown to him. Manark travelled up the levels, wondering why the Syrin Corporation had sent for him. It had been many years since he had been inside the building.

He exited the lift and recognised the person waiting for him. Rillen stood at the floor-length-window, now tinted a dusty brown to compensate for the late evening sun. Rillen must have known he was there, but did not turn. He seemed captivated by the impressive view of the city.

"Look at our world," Rillen said, his eyes fixed on the sprawling metropolis below. "This vantage point always reminds me we're scavengers in a maze."

"Scavengers...? Manark said, moving alongside him and looking out across the city. It was incredibly beautiful as the primary sun faded and the distant, less-powerful, secondary sun took its place. The rooftops radiated as if tipped with silver and gold. In front of them stood various buildings of the same height, captains of industry, but non-as powerful or as lucrative as the Syrin Corporation.

"We build, we eat, we build again," Rillen said, absently. "Time ticks away and life flows. Do we ever stop, and what would we do if we did?"

Rillen had always been this way, Manark thought. He could never understand why this man was working for this firm. He should have been working as a designer, or maybe a visual decorator, anything but a consultant.

"Sometimes I journey out, beyond the city walls, into the desert," Rillen said, his voice sounding slight. "I picture this planet before we colonised it. Just like Earth, we're dominating, invading, using up all its resources. One day we'll leave here as well, leaving behind a shell of what it was." He fell silent.

"I don't think that will happen," Manark said. "We've learnt a lot since the Earth days. We won't, hopefully, make the same mistakes."

"Sarak's edgy today," Rillen said, as if distracted by other thoughts. "It's like she's had a laser inserted up her ass."

"Thanks for the warning," Manark returned, straightening his fine coat with a delicate brush of his hand.

Rillen turned, as if bored with the view, and crossed the corridor. Manark followed the man to the large committee room door.

"Are you ready for battle?" Rillen said, his hand gripping the door handle.

Manark did not care for the consultant's choice of words. He wanted him to elaborate, but the moment had passed. It was too late. The handle turned, and the cage opened. Manark walked in. The consultant remained outside.

It was a vast room - far too large for the long conference table, he decided. There, sitting at the head of the table, was the woman herself.

She was wearing one of her infamous cream suits. It usually meant business and nothing but. Her hair sat up on top of her head, in neat rolling waves, pinned in place by various devices to give her height beyond her five-foot, six-inch frame. Legend had it she once pulled a long pin and took out a man's vision with one singular stab; but, of course, this was unsubstantiated. Her mouth, lined and crude looking, gave away nothing.

Manark approached the foot of the long desk and waited, like a puppy hoping for a treat.

Sarak sat bent over her data screen; one hand delicately held her chunky vision-goggles – which never left her head – as she examined something detailed enough to hold her attention.

A man sat on her left-hand side. A person Manark did not recognise. The man's clothing immaculate. The cut of the cloth and the way it hung like a second skin showed his standing. He had carefully slicked-back hair, feathered at the sides into neat little angles. His genetically altered chin was designer perfect.

Sarak noticed Manark and studied him for a moment. Her small eyes magnified by the thick lenses in her vision-goggles.

"Welcome," she said. "I don't think you know, Mr Davan."

The man at her side nodded his head.

"Please take a seat," Sarak continued, leaning forward and clasping her hands together. "Dr Manark, you're probably wondering why I have called on you today."

"Well, it's been a while since I worked on the Arin program," Manark said, hoping to remind her that any problem had happened long after his input.

"It has," Sarak said, trying to produce a smile but failing and only looking like she had a nose itch. "We have an issue," she said.

He breathed in. This was it. He remembered how Sarak never said the word problem – she never had problems, just issues. "Oh?" he said.

Sarak turned to her associate. "You may not know, because additional outside interaction was not highlighted, but Dr Manark here was paramount in the installation of mind stimuli and conditioning."

"Well, I worked alongside Dr Choil," Manark said, reminding her that any problem was not solely down to his own hand.

The man with the elaborate chin cleared his throat, and Sarak leaned back in her chair, giving him the floor. She had perfected the fine art of letting someone announce the trivial things. She would soon return to sharpen her knife, Manark thought.

"We have deployed a Code 6," Davan began.

"A Code 6... what is a Code 6?" Manark said.

Davan looked a little lost. "I'm sorry, I thought you were familiar with our protocol."

"It wasn't necessary at the time of his employment," Sarak interject before retreating like a shadow in a doorway. Davan continued.

"A Code 6 is a total removal of the Unit, or units."

Manark looked at the man, hoping that he had misunderstood. Hoping that the termination had not already happened. He noticed Sarak observing him through her thick lenses.

"You mean you are destroying all that work," Manark said. "How many AIs are we talking about?"

Davan's face looked almost serene as he replied. "All three of them pose a threat."

Manark swallowed. "That is crazy," he said, and slightly regretted his choice of words. His emotion was running high. For five years, he had worked on inputs and conditioning. He had watched all three of them grow beyond what anyone had considered possible. In addition, they were the first to couple with impulses – a first of their kind. He marvelled at the loss... if termination was complete.

"It became paramount to eliminate," Davan said. "They proved to be unstable."

Manark shook his head. "I'm sorry, but that is impossible."

Davan narrowed his eyes. "They were gaining individual cognitive desires beyond their coding."

"I'm sorry, but who are you?" Manark asked.

Sarak leaned forward again to speak. "Mr. Davan is our chief contributor and has had access to all files dating back to the initial drafting. In effect, he knows more about the Arin project than you or I.

Manark smiled and rubbed at his temple. "I can purchase a manual on a shuttle car and read the schematics, but it will not make me a mechanic," he said. "You say they were unstable and that they formed cognitive desires. That is not unstable, that is just development."

"Well, Mr Manark. This *development*, as you called it, jeopardised an incredibly important mission and demanded action," Davan said.

Manark was still fuming at the thought of all that wasted talent taken out at the whim of an ignorant committee.

"So you've destroyed the Arin subjects?" he said, hoping that his words might push them into admitting whether the AIs were still alive. "I'm sure that you have made duplicates based on my work. I don't see that you need me here."

It was now the time for Sarak to come forward into the fray. She hunched forward and looked at him through her goggles, large, out-dated vision creators that covered most of her upper face. He could hear the hisses and clicks as the outdated mechanics auto-focused on him.

"Of course we have others," she said. "That is not our concern. Our concern is that our elimination failed."

Now he had the truth. He breathed a little easier at hearing that the three AIs were still living. He had never heard Sarak utter such a negative word as, failed. It showed how bitter, how pathetically hostile she was towards the Arin project.

"Failed. But how?" he asked.

Sarak hit the table so hard her data comm crackled and flashed.

"That is not the issue here!" she shouted, making the man at her side recoil back into his chair. "I do not want those AIs running about with what they contain in their brains."

Manark swallowed and then needed to swallow again.

Sarak laid her hands upon the table as if steadying herself. When she spoke, her voice sounded full of Zen.

"We have called you here for your critique of the situation; think of it as your evaluation, if you will. We would like to know exactly how their parameters for change are working."

Manark felt he must ask something, and he braced himself for the consequence of his question.

"I need to know how they escaped termination. It will define the parameters."

"Very well," Sarak said. "You will have access to that information."

"And of course, your pay will be in keeping with the outstanding work you're doing," Davan said, producing the first smile of the meeting.

Manark realised, when nobody spoke, that the meeting had ended. He rose from his chair and then paused. They needed his help, so he took a chance and asked one last question.

"Why haven't you used your own schematics for the answers?"

Sarak leaned back in her chair and sighed, as if the question were tedious.

"We've inputted the figures and our great minds have raked through the data – but the answers always come back different. This project was not theirs. We need your... your skill, Doctor Manark." Then she leaned forward again and hunched over like a vulture, her eyes narrowing. "Don't over sensationalise your position here, Manark. We only need you up to a point. If you give us any difficulties, you will feel our displeasure."

Manark nodded his head and turned to leave.

"You will report here tomorrow, sign an agreement, and start your work," Sarak said as she stood.

Manark nodded his head again. He had entered the lion's cage once more, he thought.

Chapter Eight

Another plate of food lay before her. Red had been sleeping and did not see the slave-woman enter or leave. She cursed the fact, because something had happened, something far beyond her understanding.

Daddlity. Red had spoken the word repeatedly. Then something changed within her mind. A surge of activity began deep inside. Red pictured the word. Once she gave it form, it stretched out, developing other words, like thick roots exploring new soil – and these roots branched further. Red felt the framework of language grow, this time without her mental input. This activity made her tired. She lay down her head, intending to rest for a moment...

She listened and thought she detected movement. Red waited. Nothing happened.

Looking at the food made her hungry, so she reached across to the dish and took a small piece. It was only slightly warm now, so it had been here for some time. The slave would soon return for the plate.

Red had just finished her meal when the bolts of the hatch slid. This was it. She wondered how the woman would react to hearing Red's understanding of the language. Either it would make her recoil, or Red would gain a friend.

The hatch lifted. Red's heart sank when she saw the bald head come forward, with that large jewel staring at her like a third eye.

"Ah, I see my little bird is awake," he said, stepping from the hatch.

Red wondered if this man had brought her the food. She glanced at the dish and then back at the man with a questioning glance.

"Oh, don't worry, I did not visit while you slept – but I have eyes and ears everywhere," he said, inspecting the room with his gaze, evidently pleased with his power.

Red looked at him and then at the walls. He was lying. She did not know how she knew, but an inner intuition said as much.

"If I am to remain captive, can I at least know your name?" she asked.

The large man's expression changed, and he seemed genuinely embarrassed.

"Oh, little bird, I am so sorry," he said, placing one of his beefy hands on his enormous chest. "My name is Oolah."

"Well, Oolah, my name is Red…" she said, but his waving hands quashed her words. He closed his eyes, as if doing so would erase what she had said.

"No name, please. I do not want to know your name."

She realised exactly why this had distressed him. She was to be his toy – a plaything. Her name reminded him she was a person.

"So what brings you to my room today?" she asked, changing the subject.

"Oh, that is good. It is indeed your room," he chirped, and even clapped his hands together. Then he squatted down on the floor, tucking his legs in until he sat with crossed legs. Another demonstration of his agility and flexibility, Red thought.

"And you are my guest," she said and watched as his gleeful face changed.

"Let me remind you of your place, my bird," he said, his eyes peering intently. "It is I who owns your world, and it is you who is the guest." Then he took a deep breath, and a smile returned to his thin lips. "I am here to get to know you better," he said.

"Well, you already know my name, so how about…"

Red had not finished her sentence when his hand slapped hard against the side of her face. She toppled backward onto her bed and felt her cheek turn hot.

Oolah leaned forward, his hand coming out to help her as if he was genuinely sorry for his actions.

"I am so sorry. Are you hurt?" he asked, his face awash with anguish as if somebody else had slapped her. Within seconds, his face changed again. He sat back and seemed almost annoyed with her. "It wasn't my fault. You made me strike you. You were rude." He looked about. "I have given you all this… and you treat me with no respect."

She noted his breathing and his twitching eyes.

"Please forgive my foolish tongue," Red said, rising into a sitting position and bowing her head. Appeasing this man would hopefully help to mend the situation. She had woefully pushed the boundary. Red had not considered just how unstable he actually was.

Her words and the submissive way in which she bowed her head seemed to work on him. He almost chuckled with emotion. He placed his hand upon her head, as if blessing her.

"I forgive you. Now, please look at me and we can begin again."

She looked up. The side of her mouth where he had hit her was already swelling. His brow furrowed, and he put a thumb to her face. "It's such a blemish on your pretty face. I will see you have ointment before you sleep."

Red smiled, despite her discomfort.

"Well, now. I wish to know how you got here," her captor said.

"I was in a crash," she answered.

"Yes, I know that," he replied, his voice sounding impatient again. "Everyone knows that. We could hardly miss such a large shuttle coming down. I want to know who sent you and where you are from."

That was it, Red thought. This man was not interested in getting to know her at all. He wanted to know how safe it was to contain her.

A million little conundrums presented themselves. Red sifted through various answers with a speed she did not know she possessed. It was as if time had paused long enough to provide a sufficient answer.

Her biggest dilemma was fooling him with her reply. He had held others captive. He would spot an easy lie a mile away. Then other possibilities fell into place within her mind. If she said people would come, he could move her. Would this move aid her? Would another cell be more fruitful?

Red decided that this room was familiar and that it did not pose a problem. It was a place of his choosing.

This gave him a false sense of security; otherwise, he would have found a different place.

"I recall nothing other than my name," Red said, knowing that sticking close to the truth would sound better. She let her mind discard the fact that others were in the crash.

"I see no injury to your head?" he said, his facial expression one of suspicion.

"Chemical tanks ruptured, releasing gasses – I was breathing toxic fumes for some time. I guess they have had an effect.

"Oh, that might account for a loss of memory," he said, looking away, his eyes thoughtful looking as he contemplated this new information. "I suppose you will remember in time, I guess. You will tell me if you remember?" he asked, looking back at her.

"Of course, and I can't wait to know myself," she said, and again, this was true.

"Very well," he sighed. He paused long enough for Red to realise he was planning a question. "Did you not send out a distress call? I know I would."

Red nearly smiled at how transparent he was being.

"It's all very fuzzy, but I don't think there was time."

"But there will be people searching for you."

"I'm not sure. I don't even know why I was flying over this area," she admitted.

He made a small noise in the back of his throat as he considered her reply.

"Very well," he said, slapping his thigh with his hand and nimbly rising to his feet. "That is all for tonight. I will leave you to sleep."

Red nodded her head and gave him a smile. Her captor gave another chuckle and walked to the hatch. He was only half way down the steps when he paused.

"Oh, I forgot to mention. Tomorrow, when you wake, I shall come visit, and I'll have a pleasant surprise for you."

Oolah seemed rather excited at the prospect of tomorrow. His smile looked rather sinister and his face far too large for such a small mouth. His teeth, which she had not seen until now, looked underdeveloped and child-like. Red smiled back in recognition.

Content that all was well, Oolah descended, and the bolts slid closed, sealing her in.

Red let her smile fade. He was getting far too familiar. He was comfortable with her now. It would not be long before he was sitting next to her, their bodies making contact. Then the real grooming would begin. She had little time, maybe two or three visits at the most. But what could she do? She waited until she was sure that nobody was returning.

Her eyes scanned the room, but it was sparse and nothing seemed to jump out at her. She shook her head. Then she took a deep breath and banished her frustrations and swept the room again with her gaze. She considered the old info panel that lay on the slim table. It was night, which was good. There was a sufficient light to see by, and nobody would come now because it was a time of sleep. It seemed the right moment to explore the device and see what she could make of it.

CHAPER NINE

R ed had spent most of the night exploring the data comm panel. She discovered that the back panel was removable, unlike newer machines, but deep-set rivets needed to come out and she had no tools.

Removing the back panel had been her biggest hurdle and had taken a long time. She needed to break these studs without making a noise. Her mind had worked hard on the conundrum. After some time, she found an answer, although instigating it presented its own set of problems. The answer was stress. Force was too noisy, but stressing the studs might break them.

Red moved the slim black object to the edge of the desk, resting its weight on its back panel. She positioned her chest on top of the device and leaned over it, pulsing her body weight.

The device creaked. Red pressed and released her weight intermittently. She did not know how long she did this, but her chest ached from the constant pressure. Then something split.

She lifted herself from the device and inspected it. It looked intact. The back plate did not come off, but she knew that something inside had broken. Maybe a hole around a stud had fractured.

This cracking sound gave her purpose. She stood the item back on the edge of the desk and applied pressure – pulsing her body weight up and down and then, when she thought she was getting nowhere, the plate gave.

The device fell back onto the table, exposing its workings, but Red was not quick enough to catch the other section. The screen slipped to the floor and landed with a smack.

Her heart raced so fast she could feel it drumming in her ears. She waited, not daring to breathe. If someone lived in the room below, they would surely have heard.

Time slipped on. Red fought back her exhaustion. Trying to break the object had taken most of the night, and now fatigue was claiming her. But with the panel now removed, she discovered what she was working with.

The device turned out to be older than she had realised. It still used chips and wiring. At least it had its own power source. A large, primitive core-magneto sat in the middle. She traced it with her finger and that is when something happened.

Her eyes closed involuntarily. A picture presented itself. It was the machine, not just the sum of its parts – a lot more. A connection ran through her mind, as if she were part of this machine. In addition, the more she let herself connect, the more she understood its many operations.

She let her finger disengage with the object and she stood back. She breathed deeply. This was physically impossible, she told herself, but it was happening. Now she had a complete understanding of the machine, not just the problem at hand.

Her diagnostic told her that too many of the machine chips had blown. She went over to her bed and sat down to figure out if the device might serve some other purpose.

She wanted this object to be of use. Of course, she could pick it up and heave it down on Oolah as he climbed out of the trapdoor – but would it be enough to kill him? She doubted it. No, she would have to find another use for the device. A more practical use, maybe.

Red went back to the desk and put the panels back together. With a little careful handling, the object now looked whole. She returned to her bed. She fought to concentrate. Her will to problem solve was slipping, and so she let her mind drift until sleep claimed her.

· · · · ·· · ·· · ·

The fierce light made her squint. It must have been morning because the shaft of sun upon her neck was burning her skin. Shielding her eyes with her hand, she lifted herself.

Fresh food lay near. One container had liquid, the other some kind of sponge like substance. Red ate while it was still safe to do so. Her stomach groaned as she finished the dish. She drank heartily, and the influx of liquid made her feel the need for the toilet.

The tall jug stood before her. Red glanced over at the trapdoor and listened. She looked at the circular walls and decided that Oolah did not have visuals on her. Her body protested, and she reluctantly squatted over the pot. Relief was instant. After a brief moment, movement came from below, and she quickly scuttled back to her bed.

Her mind recalled Oolah's promise. She readied herself as bolts were deployed.

The black mass of unruly hair appeared as the slave woman rose from below. Red smiled, but too late –

the person had already averted her eyes. She ambled forward and headed over to the empty dishes.

"Millity breechel," Red said.

The woman stopped. Her head turned. She stood for a moment, eyes wide and frightened. She glanced over at the hatch and then at Red.

"My name is Red and I need you to help me," she said in the woman's native tongue.

"It is not safe," the woman replied.

"Our conversation will be a secret," Red said.

"He will know," the woman persisted, her expression imploring Red to stop talking. "His eyes see all."

"But not here... I have checked," Red said, coming forward to touch her hand.

Just like before, this sudden connection made the slave recoil.

"I mean you no harm," Red said.

"Touch is forbidden. Only the master can..." the woman faltered, quickly averting her eyes, not daring to finish the sentence.

"There have been many before me, but today this must stop," Red said.

The slave shook her head and took a step back. Her once animated face now looked frozen with fear. Her conditioning quickly shut off that part of her mind she used for independent thought. The woman was shaking her head as if Red were forcing her to face something taboo or impossible.

"Please. You are my only hope. My name is Red. I will help you once you have helped me."

The woman stooped and picked up the dishes and then crossed back to the hatch.

"My name is Red. You are my only hope."

The slave was already disappearing down through the opening in the floor. Then the hatch slammed shut, leaving Red alone.

Chapter Ten

M anark entered the Syrin building carrying a new scan card. It was morning, and he had not slept well. No amount of credits was worth returning here, he told himself as he contemplated his day ahead.

The desk personnel scanned his card and ushered him to the lift.

"The lower sectors are open to you. Sub-levels one to five," security said. "The service lift will operate on this card but will not access higher levels unless you're given an override."

Manark nodded. He remembered the drill from his last period of employment. He could not wait to enter the lift and separate himself from the lobby person – if he was an actual person – it was hard to tell in a place that was so proficient in droid manufacture. The

Syrin Corporation had many avenues involving droid production - More than Real, being their motto. The lift door slid shut. Manark managed a smile before the security man vanished from view – the security man did not return the courtesy.

The lift quickly reached the first sub-level. The doors opened to reveal a well-lit and well-ventilated corridor. People spent an awful amount of time down here, and Syrin took every step to make it as comfortable as possible. Large wall monitors displayed vast fields of waving wheat, even though farming crops were an indoor operation on Majarri. Still, the image was restful and induced a sense of calm.

Manark followed a sign. The layout came back to him. He had walked this corridor many times from one lab to another. He waked past a rest area. Circular seating ran around a small fountain. The seating was empty. Too early in the day for many and too much on the agenda for others. Room B3 came into view and he stopped.

His scan card gave access – the door gently swished open. Manark entered the changing room and went to a locker matching the number on his scan card. Again, he swiped, and the locker opened. He took out the pale blue clothing. A towel hung from a peg. He took this too and undressed. Then he placed his clothing into the locker and went through a door on his left. He placed his towel and his lab clothing on a nearby bench and stepped into a booth. A single button protruded from the wall. He pressed it. A reddish foam came from various hoses, coating him with a sticky substance. Then tiny blasts of warming air evaporated the foam. Decontamination, even at data level, was paramount. Surgical levels on the next floor had hours dedicated to deep cleaning.

Manark quickly dressed in the pale blue clothing and put his towel down a chute. He walked to the end of the room and swiped his card again. He entered the first lab.

The air was fresh and temperature perfect. Six people were going about their busy schedules. Two of them were gazing down through microscopes, their info pads waiting beside them for their findings. They seemed far too distracted to look up at this new arrival.

Manark walked over to the wall and picked up an info pad. He activated it with his card. He carried the device to a flexi-screen. A person with slicked-back hair came towards him carrying a Digi-board. Her walk was a gentle shuffle, her blue overshoes made a gentle noise, like paper against stone.

"Are you Manark?" she asked.

"That is correct," he said, putting out his free hand.

"My name is Doctor Treece," she said. "I'm the Lab 3 coordinator. I can direct questions that you may have to the right channels."

She had a firm grip and, again, Manark wondered if she were human. Her face was pleasing, her eye colour quite distinct, making her visually appealing, but this was a trait of the company. *More than Real*, meant just that. They did not manufacture picture perfect people, but visually genuine people, complete with moles, scars, and even non-symmetrical features. People had grown bored with immaculate model-perfect synthetics, even in the pleasure industry. Realistic was the new fake.

"I'm here to diagnose information connected to the Arin project," he said.

The woman smiled. "No need to explain. I understand your function here. If I can help with anything, then just ask," she said with a smile, extending a hand towards a free area.

He took a seat and waited for the woman, or android, carrying her Digi-board to walk away. Then he turned his attention to the large panel. He inserted his card into the device and watched the screen come to life. On the side was a tiny clip that he attached to his ear. A voice spoke to him.

"Welcome to the mother board A-frame 2." The voice continued to list the areas that A-frame 2 covered. Manark touched the screen and skipped the intro. The screen turned pale-green and the Syrin logo appeared, sparkling like a fiery phoenix.

His finger traced down a long list until he found the word Arin. Then he chose a subheading and then another, gaining deeper and deeper levels until he found stats and bio recordings.

For the next couple of hours, he digested the data, occasionally working on his small data-pad and then looking back at the screen. He marvelled at how advanced the three units had become. He worked with them through five generative stages before Syrin ended his contract in a premature but satisfactory way. However, Syrin had taken them past segments 6 and 7 and into 8. Their bio graphs and algorithms presented themselves and Manark caught up with the last few years of growth. It was beyond anything that he could have perceived. They had developed exponentially. They no longer resembled what he remembered. Especially their mind development. These new inputs intrigued him. They only had code names, and when he asked the main frame for more information, his level of clearance would not grant him access.

Manark pressed a wall button and within a moment, the woman known as Treece came shuffling neatly towards him; her smile even more welcoming than before.

"I need access to...," he accessed his data pad and read out three input codes.

The woman quickly tapped her pad and then looked at him.

"What you are requesting is listed above your operating code."

"I know it is, but it is paramount to my investigation."

She considered him for a moment, her bright eyes unblinking, and then her smile returned, making him believe that this woman *was* a machine. Either that or her training had turned her into the next best thing.

"I will check to see if we can grant you this information," she said, turning on the spot and walking away. He watched her go, inspecting the swish of her silk-like-skirt. Weighing up if the walk was natural or mechanical. He was undecided. Her mannerisms still made him think she was an AI, but then again, some people were robotic in their mannerisms, anyway.

He turned back to the screen and explored information about physical dexterity. He studied what was a detailed analysis of the three AIs' abilities to perform in extreme circumstances. It was all quite remarkable.

A short moment later, a gentle voice in his earpiece stopped him reading and announced his upgrades, including access to the three codes that he had asked for. He looked away from the screen, down the aisle, towards Treece, and waved appreciatively. She spotted him and waved back.

Manark accessed this additional information. "Right; what have you been up to since I was last here?" he said under his breath. Then he saw the new avenue that Syrin had taken – and it shocked him. What they had put these three units through went beyond the laws of ethics. Even synthetic life-forms had governing bodies that controlled corporate and private operations. That was Syrin all over, he thought, acting like a god and ignoring the foundational rules of the planet. Putting that aside, he could not believe that these organically built individuals could survive such inputs. It was unheard of, even in times such as these. The developments that he explored were years ahead of anything. Far beyond what great minds could envisage, let alone implement.

He leaned back on the stool, the micro backrest taking his weight. He breathed heavily and rubbed his forehead with the palm of his hand. Then, out of the corner of his eye, he noticed a small subheading. He leaned forward, peering intently at the heading that he had overlooked. There was another code. Manark touched it, and the voice denied him his wish. He tapped again to be sure he had read the reaction correctly. The system denied him access, and he sat there, mystified. He thought for a moment.

This code restriction was not a mistake. If this information remained closed, then they did not want him knowing what it contained, despite his need for analysis. No. Whatever the reasoning, he would not push to find out. He could continue with his investigation and maybe piece together things from different logs, join the binary and replace the strands of understanding. Just what they had done to these AIs, he could only speculate – but his gut told him he did not want to know.

Chapter Eleven

The hatch was opening again. Red watched as Oolah's bald head rose like a pale rock.

"It is a fine morning," he said, coming out of the hole and standing to straighten his back. He was wearing a lime green cloth with a red trim finish – and he was carrying something.

Red did not speak. The failed connection with Oolah's slave was still playing on her mind. No matter how she tried to soothe her overactive thoughts, the feeling of containment was thicker than ever. Her hope was dwindling. All she had was this fat oaf and the promise of things that she did not dare contemplate.

"My little bird has lost her singing voice," he said as he once again squatted down on the floor, his legs easily folding into a comfortable position. He put the cylindrical object down beside him without looking at it.

"I'm not your little bird," Red said, her mind in no mood for this charade.

Oolah carefully brought his hand out and gently gripped her chin. He turned her face so that he could inspect her. "Oh, those injuries are doing well. They have nearly gone," he said.

Red got the message. Bruises could vanish, but they could easily reappear.

"So how are you today?" she said with a sigh, her eyes squinting from the harsh shaft of light.

Her words made him light up, and he nodded his head.

"Oh, I hardly slept," he said. Red suddenly wondered if he had heard the crash from her breaking the data-cover. "I have been so excited about today," he added.

Red did not share in his excitement. His pleasure was surely her pain. Time was running out. He would only wait so long to sample the new fruit.

"I've been for a delightful walk in my garden. Oh, you should see it," he said. "But then, if you are good, you *may* get to see it. We can stroll thought the grounds and make good this glorious sunlight."

"How does your garden grow in such a harsh environment?" she asked.

Oolah looked rather taken at her sudden interest. He nodded his head like a proud father. "You may well ask. The answer is very simple. Solar 3 lies above a vast watering hole. Yes, can you believe it?"

Red looked at him, analysing his words. "But the people of Solar 3 are drinking synthetic water. The city is pretty much barren," she said.

He looked at her with a blank face, as if her observations were nothing. Oolah seemed genuinely removed from the notion, as if he had not contemplated the fact before.

"Oh, well," he said. "Not everyone can have this water. If we rationed it out, there would not be a watering hole – at least not enough to sustain such a vast city. I'm doing the city a great favour by preserving it."

His words shocked her. He was draining this area beyond the wall while the city consumed substandard liquid. They lived in a dust bowl while this man walked beneath his green canopy and breathed in his exotic flowers. It was criminal.

"Do you not agree with me?" he said, tilting his head and waiting for her reply.

She sensed that this was another step forward in their development. He was now testing her alliance. He awaited her answer, and if it did not meet his approval, then who knew how he would react. She would have to be cunning.

"Well, you can't make everyone happy, can you?" she said.

He was still staring at her, deciding if her convictions were true – his fingers drummed on the long tube beside him.

"Oh, I nearly forgot," he said, taking to his feet and holding out the tube like a precious sceptre. "This is the reason for my sleepless night."

Oolah passed her the object. It looked like it contained something to dress the room, a flag or a banner.

Red removed the lid and pulled at a piece of cloth. It was a fine dress. The material felt airy, like the cloth she was wearing, only lighter. It was lemon in colour and had a certain sparkle to it. Along with the garment, was something resembling a long piece of rope? This other item made her heart flutter. The thought of bondage made her nearly recoil.

"That is the belt," he said, his smile gentle – proud even. "An unusual addition. It is a little stiffer than most belts. You can tie it around your waist, but it is firm enough to be used to style your hair – or a thousand and one different applications."

He spoke casually, and without emphasis, but she knew exactly what he was implying.

"What is it made from?" she asked, taking a deep breath and inspecting the belt. It was pliable enough, like a belt, but ridged enough to grip an object.

"Oh, you're so clever," he said. "You can spot something of incredible sophistication. It's very expensive, I may add." He came closer and took the belt from her hands. "Beneath its material covering, lies long striations of metal thread running along the entire length."

Oolah dropped the belt and took two steps back. "Well, I think you should wear such a fine gift. Dress now so that I may marvel at its beauty."

Red looked at him. The cheeks of her face flush. Her eyes searched the room for somewhere to change, but there was nowhere.

"Oh, come along now," he said. "We are past all this. We are friends." His eyes narrowed and his small mouth puckered and seemed to vanish all together. "Dress in the fine clothing I have brought for you," he said.

She swallowed and her body trembled. Then an inner anger filled her, and she defiantly grabbed at her own clothing and slid it over her head in one swift movement. She stood before him for a second or two, angrily letting his eager eyes ravage her body. She did this to satisfy his curiosity and to defy his wish to see the costume on her, even for a slight moment.

Oolah's eyes widened as he gazed upon her nakedness. He fought to control his reactions. Then Red bent down and picked up the dress and belt. She slipped on this new clothing and then tied the stiff chord about her waist. She waited.

Oolah's eyes suddenly relaxed, and he looked down. Then he was turning. He walked back to the open hatch, leaving her standing there.

He was half way down the stairs when he said, without looking at her, "Change back into your rags."

The hatch closed and Red felt her anger reach a new level. She clenched her teeth and stamped her naked foot. How dare he, she thought. Then she realised the psychology, and she forced herself not to react further. He had walked away as if she were nothing. Using the word "Rags" reminded her of her standing. Her defiant strip had meant nothing to him.

She had played a dangerous game and now realised she was dancing with fire. She had stood for too long, letting him drink up her nakedness. His curiosity seemed satisfied, but only visually. It did nothing to quash his want for touch.

Chapter Twelve

R ed sighed and absently shuffled over to the window. The walled city, with its bustle of market tents and dusty red buildings, lay before her. Soft tendrils of smoke from food venders wafted up, tainting the blue, cloudless sky with its filthy colour. The slim window on the other side of the tower held no view, because a vast jungle blocked everything, including the light. Nobody knew of her existence. The thought terrified her. The tower was the perfect prison. Not even sounds came or went.

She inspected the garment. It meant nothing to her. Despite its fine tailoring, the garment seemed soiled by its intentions. She took it off and threw it towards the small table. She contemplated destroying it, but she knew the consequences of such an act. With reluctance, she redressed in her original rags.

Her familiar dress felt better.

Bolts scraped. Red took a step back as the hatch opened. The woman had returned. She was holding a bowl of fresh water. Her eyes found Red, and they swapped glances. Red said nothing. She hoped her sudden silence was enough to make the woman feel guilty for not rushing to her aid.

The slave carefully crossed the room and placed the bowl down on the floor.

"What is that for?" Red asked, again, in the woman's own dialect.

The slave looked at her with a puzzled expression. "Why, it is to drink," she said.

Red went over and kicked the bowl over, spilling the contents over the stone floor.

"Why do you want to keep me alive? Is it not enough that I am to suffer at his hand?"

The woman looked at Red for a moment and then down at the bowl.

"You must drink, you must stay alive," she whispered.

Red gritted her teeth. "I must stay alive... to be his toy?" she said. "You want me to suffer, day after day. You are just as bad as he."

The woman shook her head. "That is not true..."

"Yes, it is. You have the power to help me and yet you do nothing but keep me watered."

"I have to serve him. I have to do what he says," she said, her dark eyes wide and pleading.

Breathing in deeply, Red controlled her emotions. The woman was only doing her job, but Red had little choice.

"How about I tell him you dropped this bowl?"

The slave looked at Red, and her mouth hanging open, her hands rubbing together with uncertainty.

"Please, you must not. It did not happen this way. It was you who spilt the water."

"Do you think he will believe you?" Red asked. "And even if he believed it was me, he would blame you for allowing this to happen. What will he do to you?"

The woman's scrawny chest rose and fell.

"Please," she said, falling to her knees and holding out her hands. "I am old and he will beat me."

"And what will he do to me if I stay here, waiting, drinking his water and wearing his fancy clothing? What awaits me?"

Red grabbed the woman's shoulders and made her meet her gaze.

"Help me. We can defeat him. If you let me escape, I will not run. I will kill him and rid us both of this burden."

Red looked deep into the women's eyes and saw a flicker of hope. They were both powerless, but together they could overturn him. The slave looked at her with weary eyes and blinked away a tear.

"You think you can defeat him?" the slave asked.

"I know I can defeat him," she said with as much conviction as she could muster.

The woman still looked uncertain.

"What is your name?" Red asked.

"Janna," the woman said, looking mystified. Evidently, it had been a long time since anyone had asked her name.

"My name is Red."

The woman repeated her name, slowly digesting its sound. The more she stared at Red's enthusiastic expression, the more her face came to life. Her eyes sparkled with moisture. Then she nodded her head. "I will help you escape if you make him gone."

Red let out her breath and laughed. Now she too had tears in her eyes. "You are a wonderful woman, Janna."

Janna turned her head and looked like she was planning something. Red moved over to the hatch. She peered down. It was her first sighting of the area below.

"No," the woman said, pulling her about. "That way is not for you. Too risky – another does his bidding. There is a sensor that will know how many pass through." Then the slave looked over to the window.

"I will bring you something to break that pane. You can jump to the tree and climb down the vines."

Red moved over to the window. The nearest tree was about six feet away, and she did not believe she could make it. She turned to say this to the woman, but Janna was already disappearing back down the steps, pulling the trapdoor behind her.

Holding on to the feeling of hope, Red paced the room. It was not an easy jump to make, but her options were as slim as Janna's arms. If she did not leap into the tree, then maybe she could grab hold of a branch as she fell. It was a whole heap better than lying around waiting for Oolah to reappear and place his greasy hands all over her.

· · · · ●· ● ● · · ·

Too much time had elapsed, Red told herself. Maybe the slave had changed her mind. Red reminded herself that Janna had many tasks to perform. The more that the slave went about her business, the more chance that their plan might work.

The hatch opened, and the Janna clambered out with another jug. She looked back and listened before coming into the centre of the room. Then she reached inside the narrow neck of the pot and took out a long metal instrument. The implement looked charred and covered with fine traces of ashes.

"Strike the corner of the glass," the woman said.

Wasting no time at all, Red moved over to the large window and turned the poker so that the thick handle was pointing at the glistening glass.

She looked at the desk. Her new clothing still lay there. She picked up the fine garment, scrunched it into a ball, and held it against the glass to soften the sound. She issued a quick test tap. The cloth worked well. She hit the glass again and then a third time, but nothing happened.

"With more force," the woman said, her hands gesticulating wildly, her eyes as big as eggs.

Red nodded her head, brought the poker back, and hit the widow again, this time with more force, but still the thick glass held. She removed the cloth and used both hands to wield the poker. The metal hit the glass but did no damage. Red even leaned forward to examine the glass.

"The glass is too tough," Red said, turning to look at her accomplice – then she gasped. Oolah was standing half in and half out of the floor hatch.

"That is Tanusian glass," he said.

The old woman turned and screamed.

"The compound is heavily reinforced, making it virtually unbreakable," he calmly informed as he moved into the room.

Oolah did not say a word as he grabbed the slave's shoulder and pulled her to him. He looked her squarely in the face for a second, and then tossed her down the steps. Janna fell through the hole in the floor like a limp pillow and landed with a thud. Oolah looked down at her. "I will be down to deal with you," he said, his voice amazingly calm under the circumstances. Red noted that there was no response and feared the worst.

"No." Red said, backing away from the window. She held the poker out before her. At least she now had a weapon, she told herself.

"You will not hurt me," the man said, striding towards her with determination.

When he was close enough, Red thrust the weapon forward. Oolah skilfully twisted and the item passed by, scraping his shoulder but doing no damage. His hands dashed out, his grip tight as he grabbed her.

He pried the poker from her hands. She cried out as the weapon slipped from her fingers.

"So you want to play rough, do you?" he said. He turned the poker around in his hand so that the thick handle was protruding, and he whacked it against her middle. Red bent over, the air leaving her lungs. She cried out when a second blow connected with her shoulder. Another blow made her crumple and fall back onto her bed. He came into view, towering over her, slamming blow after blow with his new weapon.

The man was in a frenzy as he beat at her limbs. He even stamped on her hand at one point, but the mattress helped take the blow. Still, when he stopped, Red felt crippled. She pulled her arms about her and lay still, her body shaking with pain, pulsed with heat.

"Do you like this game?" he said, his voice calm and curt.

She lifted her throbbing head and watched him move back to the hatch.

"I have other tasks to address and then I will return," he said, glancing down the steps. "Please dress in the new clothing that I have provided. It is time for us to be friends. And if I do not see you dressed in the finery, I will show no mercy."

She watched him descend, and the hatch closed. Then he shouted, "Get up." Then again, "Get up, filthy wretch." Janna was probably unconscious, or worse. Oolah uttered his frustration and then he was panting. It sounded like he was shifting her body. Then silence returned to the lower area.

Red lay her head back down. A wave of sickness knotted her burning stomach. Hot tears filled her eyes. This was it, she thought. She could not defend herself. Her body was of no use. The pain and bruising was too much and the room impossible. To add to that, her only aid now lay in the hands of her jailer.

Hope felt like something other people possessed. All she could wish for was his compassion, as much as this man could possess compassion. That meant wearing his silly costume. She did not know how she was going to suffer that belt around her delicate middle. Then she considered the item for a moment and a new thought entered her head. She had nothing left to give and nothing left to lose. Her mind clung to this slither of an idea. She got up, summoning the energy she needed to stand.

Chapter Thirteen

M anark sat with two tubes of compressed food from the vending machine and watched people as they passed.

Syrin had several parks, carefully sculpted to optimise relaxation. Manark could have opted to take his breakdown in the sublevels. They had a synthetic park down there, complete with wildlife: all units, of course, but programmed with schematics down to the last flinch. Therefore, if you spotted some kind of wildlife, you actually thought you were seeing a wonder of nature.

He contemplated sitting inside, but he needed to see the sun, feel its light, and smell genuine air, not the synthetic machine oxygen of the lower levels. Machines and manufacturing. It was all about the servant of humans. Then he considered the three rogue synthetics. Could he still label them as synthetic or AIs? He decided he could not, but could not, decide on a more fitting term.

How many of the people who walked past were real? He could not tell. There was a time that you could, but that time had passed. A painting so detailed as to fool the eye became a photograph despite its medium.

Manark's mind thought again about the three AIs... and about that code. He shook his head, trying to rid himself of the thought. It was like saying to a child – do not look under that box. The box became everything. Were scientists just children at heart, their minds always lost in wonder, no matter how much knowledge they learnt?

He wanted to admit something to himself, but he shook his head, trying to ignore the idea. A woman walked past and smiled at him, distracting his mind. He smiled back. He remembered something one of the Syrin people had told him. Syrin actually made several droids that walked about, openly flirting as they went. Manark had dismissed this as nonsense, but the man had insisted. He said there were male and female bots walking around, smiling, and giving people the eye. It made the company more interesting to work for.

The woman in question turned her head as she walked away. She was stunning, with her carefully sculpted short black hair and wide, well-painted mouth. Her eyes looked playful. Then she was changing course, cutting through the oncoming flow until he lost sight of her. Now he could believe it. He knew he was not an attractive man, and at fifty, with his greying beard and his heavy jowls, he was a tough sell.

His mind, now free to wonder, returned to his conundrum. He rubbed one of his sweating palms across his thigh. What he was contemplating was dangerous. Beyond dangerous, he told himself. Just do your job, take the pay, and get the hell out. He was freelance now, so he could pick his work. He could not understand why he had accepted this job in the first place – yes, he did. It was a question of vanity and ego. The initial mind programing was all his. He did not want someone scrutinising his part in the development with his or her thoughts and assessments.

He told himself what he was proposing would not work. It had been years since he was in the system. Still, it did not stop him from wondering about the possibility.

He drummed his fingers on the arm of the bench. What did he have to lose? Again, his mind had the answer. The Mainframe would know that he had tried his old password, from his pastime with the firm. It would log his access request. He thought on – wrestling with the dilemma. How many people worked here? Three, four thousand? Could they watch every input? His mind reasoned that if his old password, with all its access qualifications, was still active, then the mainframe would not even log his usage. As far as the mainframe knew, he was just another worker. That hidden code would open up like a flower.

Manark activated his portable data pad and dialled his home access. Checking communications and vita-logic announcements were not only acceptable but also encouraged. Without moving his head, he checked the scene ahead, and then, before he talked himself out of it, quickly tapped the screen.

He ran a scan for files containing his Syrin work and found several. Then he found a subheading with the label, *Work access*. He scanned further, wafting through his old dock-signings and personal info. There it was – his override setup from his previous time with the firm. He had stored them in case his card became lost. Without pausing for contemplation, he copied the file to his data collection page and closed the link.

He walked back inside the building feeling like a criminal. His mind was sure at any moment guards would arrive to carry him off to wherever they interviewed digital electro-threats. After travelling down in the lift, he repeated his earlier process of decontamination. Once germ free, he joined the lab and felt as if a thousand eyes were watching. It was busier than before. The woman was still at her post, helping someone. She looked up but did not react.

Slipping his card back into the panel, he accessed the same screen. He gazed at the elusive code. Clicking on it again made the screen flash. The word denied appeared. Manark looked about and then typed the nine-digit override. The screen changed, and he was in. His old access code was active.

Manark ran his hand through his hair. He marvelled as rows upon rows of headings appeared. The first heading intrigued him. It read, "Arin Updates." Manark read, and his stomach turned. The information was more than he could have imagined. The new generation of inputs was fantastical. He gasped aloud.

He read another file and then a third. The last file he read had the physical data. Biorhythms presented themselves. Another section had a list of drugs that it took to sustain them throughout the process. It was an extensive list. A human body might not have survived such additions.

Manark was clicking on a visual diary when he heard his name called. Turning around, he saw two men looking at him. His mouth went dry. His hand extracted the card from the machine. The screen behind him went blank.

"Dr Manark, we would like to speak with you," one of them said. They were wearing the same lab clothing as he, but this was just a requirement of the area. He noted the dark uniform beneath – these people were security. Manark felt his chest tighten.

"Can I help you?" he asked.

"We need you to come with us," the other operative said.

Manark gestured at the screen behind him. "I have my work to do. I have data to process."

"The upper levels have requested you," the guard said.

"What for?" Manark asked.

"The request is not open for discussion. Come with us right away," the man furthered.

Manark stood up. His legs felt heavy. He looked around and saw the Lab coordinator looking at him with a blank expression. Had she reported him? Had she accessed his screen, being an overseer? Could it have been the mainframe with its code analysis? Manark had no option but to follow the two men.

Chapter Fourteen

R ed's body had protested when she first stood. As she moved about, the only actual pain came from her elbow, which had taken a direct hit. She paced about, swinging her limb until the pulsing slowed to a dull, gentle thud. Every movement she took was a step towards rehabilitation. She marvelled at how responsive, how resourceful her body was being.

Content that she now had some kind of articulation, she shuffled over to the old data screen. It sat there, with its back still carefully propped in place.

Red reached around with her good arm and removed the panel. She turned the screen around and looked for the dynamo. This kind of dynamo had an inbuilt electrical impulse. It was dormant, yet still serviceable. What it needed was a trigger, something that could draw the current.

Picking up the belt with its metal fibres, she slid off her dress. She noted how easily her arm was moving. She touched her legs. The bruises were there, but instead of pain, there was only a numbness. The man had beaten her hard with a metal poker, and now her damage was only slight. It made little sense, but she was relieved to find that her body was healing.

Red was still inspecting her body when she reminded herself that Oolah had promised to return. She would not disappoint him. She dressed in her new costume and grabbed her old one, wrapping the cloth around her hand several times. Then she took hold of the belt and wrapped the end around the thick protruding disk of the magneto. Several sparks shot out. Good, she told herself. Even after all this time, it was still holding power.

Red was careful to pick up the other end of the belt with her bandaged hand, the soft cloth acting as a shield. She looked at the chord, which had now become a conductor.

She waited. Red positioned herself between the desk and the trap door, hiding the data panel she had laid flat on the desk top. She did not have to wait long. Her captor's footfalls echoed through her beating heart as he climbed the steps. He was still angry. His heavy-footed approach told her as much. This was it. Time to face the bull.

Oolah came up from the hatch and showed surprise at seeing her standing there. He paused at the top, one foot still on the step, the other placed firmly on the floor. He stared for a moment and Red could see his anger reducing. His eyes, drinking up the sight of her, dressed and ready, gleamed with an eager anticipation.

"Oh, I see you have come to your senses," he said, stepping forward. He smiled. "Oh, but you're not completely ready," he said. "You seem to have forgotten your belt?"

Red shook her head. "I have tried, but there's something wrong with it," she replied, keeping her voice low and her expression a mask of frustration.

Oolah came forward to fix the problem. His hands reached out towards her.

"The problem is with the tip," she said, holding the end up for him to see, hoping that he would not have the time to inspect the item.

Oolah bent his head forward to gain a better view. He spotted her bound hand, and he frowned, but it was too late.

Red lifted the belt up and thrust it forward until it connected with Oolah's jewelled forehead. The jewel sat within a metal clasp. The effect was instant. Sparks flew out as the two materials connected.

Oolah did not even have time to utter his surprise. His head shook. His eyes slid back in their sockets and his entire body trembled. For a moment, Red thought he would grab hold of her, making the current run between them, but he stood frozen. Then the current died.

His eyes continued to roll, and slithers of saliva ran from the corner of his tiny mouth. He toppled forward. He tried to move his arms, but they were slow, and he fell down with a slap.

Red wasted no time. She turned him on his back and looked into his eyes.

"I'm going to lock you in this tower. The windows will hold you. I can testify to that. When I get down stairs, I will find out if you have killed your servant. If you have, I will burn this tower. If she is still alive, then I will spare you, but it will be down to your friend if she feeds you."

Oolah's eyes were flickering back into life, and Red knew it was time to leave. She searched his pockets and found a tiny object. The device let the bearer pass through the electronic hatch shield. She found the key and moved over to the hatch. She was half way down when the big man turned his head. Red continued her descent and pulled the hatch closed behind her.

"You cannot hold me!" he shouted. "No tower can hold me!"

The area below contained large storage crates. Some containers were open, their contents spilling across the floor. Dried food goods – mostly seeds and grains, rested on the ground. Other containers held cloth and farming equipment. The clutter nearly concealed the round walls. Red felt her heart lift when she spotted another staircase. These stairs were wider and of better construction than the hatch-steps. Red continued, not knowing what she would find. Unlike the previous floor, this area was sparse, holding just a couple of items of discarded furniture and a rather dusty looking set of potting containers – and still the stairs continued on down.

Red reached the last step and saw Janna. The slave had pulled herself up against the wall. Her lips looked swollen and bloodied, but still she tried to smile. She cradled her arm, and her dress lay tattered and decorated with speckles of blood.

"Are you alright?" Red asked, going to her and placing a reassuring hand on the woman's shoulder.

The woman opened her mouth. "Is he dead?" she asked, her eyes still filled with fear.

"No, I spared him," Red said, brushing a strand of hair from the woman's face. "Do not worry – I locked him in the top room. He can no longer hurt you."

Janna's body relaxed. Red noticed a single tear trace her cheek. The slave had spent a long time in service to this man. Now she could finally rest, if only for a little while.

"Can you walk?" Red asked. Janna managed a crooked smile, despite her wounds. With Red's help, she could stand.

They went through to a back room containing a table and chairs. Red stopped when she noticed the cage.

A boy stood in that cage, no older than eight years of age. He considered Red with his wild looking eyes.

Janna went over to a wall and took a large scan card to the lock. One swipe made the device open.

The boy cowered back over to the far wall. The thin woman bent down and beckoned the boy.

"Who is he?" Red asked.

Janna turned her head. "This is my son," she said. Then she nodded towards the ceiling. "It is also his son," she added.

Red felt a wave of repulsion. The fiend at the top of the tower was no more human than a scavenging sand-dog.

"It is alright; this lady has freed us," the woman said.

The boy looked at Red, not daring to believe. Then he ran to his mother, and they embraced.

Red looked at the boy's pen, with its small stool and table, and could not believe that a person could contain people in this way.

"This is Neeper."

"It's a fine name," Red said, smiling.

Red reminded herself that they were not out of danger. She asked Janna if there were others here and Janna said that there was just one other, a slave-woman, like herself, who was out in the city, running errands. Red questioned further, asking if anyone was due to visit. Janna replied that a provisions provider came once a day with food. She smiled and said that she dealt with the man, not Oolah.

"That is good," Red said. "Tonight we will all sit and eat and work out a plan." She looked down at the boy. "How does that sound, Neeper?"

Janna cried again. "You have saved our life," she said. Red cried as well and for a moment, they all stood, not daring to believe the ordeal was over.

CHAPTER FIFTEEN

T he other slave returned from the city with a basket of ointment. Tonight, there would be no such pampering for Oolah. When this woman, who had a deep scar running from her eye down to her jaw, heard the news of Oolah's demise, she dropped the basket. Her hand came to her mouth as she exhaled a long, victorious cry. She even looked up at the ceiling with a broad smile spreading across her mouth.

They gathered a fine array of foods and liquids and feasted well. With their stomachs full and their eyes shining with contentment, they plotted.

"So what do you want to do?" Red asked. She noted their empty expressions. "Can I make a suggestion?" Red added. The two women nodded their heads. "I take it that Oolah is not one for going to the city."

Janna explained how he only visited once a month and that he was not due again for some time.

"That is good," Red smiled. "You have time to escape."

She watched as they swapped frightened glances.

"But where would we go? What would we do for a living? We are too old to start again," Janna said.

Red nodded her head and thought. They had no means to support themselves and no social standing to get aid.

"Oolah had a position, did he not?" Red asked. They told her he was one of three custodians. "What are the other people like within this wooded area?" Red furthered.

The women looked at each other. "They keep themselves to themselves. The people here are ancient. They never visit."

"So what happens when one dies? Who would be *your* next master?"

Now Red saw their faces light up.

"That would be Perliss," Janna said, her face suddenly bright with hope. "Perliss is a good man. Twice he came here to check on us. He asked us how we were." Then her face dropped. "Oolah had already promised violence if we told how he treated us. We bathed and wore better clothing on the day Perliss visited."

"So your new master would be kind to you?"

"Yes, he is a good-hearted man. Oolah did not like him. He said he was weak."

Red smiled. "You must bring him to me."

Janna sent the other woman back out and time slowed beyond measure. Red wondered if she was ever going to return, but return she did.

Perliss was a slender man who walked with a limp. Most of his weight rested on his carbon staff. He had cold black hair and his smile was gentle. The man paused long enough to take Red's hand and shake it. Red could tell he was a people's man.

"But where is Oolah?" he asked. Red shook her head and asked him to take a seat while Janna brought him the finest of waters.

"If you are going to tell me he's had an accident, then I will not believe you," the man said, lifting the drink to his mouth but never letting his eyes stray.

"I would not insult your inelegance," Red replied. "I will, if you will indulge me, tell you the facts."

Perliss listened intently. Red told her story of capture and imprisonment. Perliss did not interrupt, but several times, he nodded his head in disbelief and tutted. After her own story, she explained about the other people in the house and of their plight. Then Red sat silently, as did Perliss.

The man rubbed a finger around the rim of his drinking tube and sat thinking. He briefly glanced at Janna, who nodded her head as if to say that what he heard was true.

"I believe you. I believe you all," the man said, leaning back in his chair. "And you have locked Oolah securely in the room upstairs?"

"He is," Red replied. Then she grew curious. "What makes you believe us?" she asked.

Perliss leaned forward. "Two things make me believe you," he said. "The first is Janna. I have known her for many years. She used to come to market once a week in the old days." Perliss took Janna's hand and kissed it. "I heard rumours about Oolah. These rumours made me wonder about his household, so I came here to see for myself. Had I known the truth…" he trailed off.

"So what are we to do?" Red asked.

"That is the big question," he replied. "We cannot make him accountable. He is too powerful and too many owe him favours. No, we must be cunning."

Red saw him glance again at Janna. He was still holding her hand, fondly. That is when Red really noticed how much this man was fond of the woman.

"You know," he said, glancing over at Red. "Janna was one of the most desirable woman in all of Solar 3. If she had been a free person, her life would have been so different. Of course, things were not like that. But if I had known, all those years ago, how she was being mistreated, I would have crushed Oolah with my own hands."

Red looked at Janna and then back to Perliss. "You could not see her demise – her change?" she asked. "Her frail look and cuts and bruises must have been a giveaway."

"It is hard for you to know, but I did not see her – sometimes, many months had passed. I have seen many a woman reduced to nothing in the service of a man. Hands become brittle and work can... dry out a person. But then Janna stopped coming to the city."

"It is true," Janna said. "Oolah grew tired of me forgetting things from his list. I got careless."

"The whole of Solar 3 was careless," Red said, angry that such a place could consume a person until they were nothing – a commodity that had no voice of their own.

Perliss dropped Janna's hand and placed his own on Red's. "I promise you this. To the city, it will appear nothing has changed for Janna; but she will have her freedom within these grounds to live out her life in comfort."

Red studied him for a moment. "Can you really promise that?"

Perliss nodded his head. "Oolah is a big man and if he should have an accident... a fatality of some description, then I would be naturally first in line to resume his duties."

Red breathed a sigh of relief.

"Very well," she said. "What are we to do first?"

"You must take me to Oolah. Please fetch my cane. My legs are bad and the stairs are many."

A moment later, Red walked behind Perliss as he ambled slowly up the many steps. She had to assert a certain amount of patience as the man took the stairs, swinging his frail legs forward as they ascended.

The woman with the scar did not want to go with them, but Janna followed and her expression was grave, as if she were about to confront the monster that had stolen so much of her life.

Finally, they reached the hatch. Then Perliss turned to her. "I must go alone," he said. "Wait at the foot of these stairs, but stay out of sight until I have been successful in what I must do. Can you do this?" he asked.

Red thought for a moment, not exactly sure what this frail man could achieve. She nodded her head reluctantly. She passed Perliss the small device that allowed a person to pass through the shield; then she moved back, as did Janna. Red watched as the man took the first of the steep steps. Then she glanced about. Several boxes stood in a simple stack, and she quickly found something amongst them she could use as a weapon should things go wrong. She picked up a long pole with a hook on the end. Janna looked at it and she, too, searched the boxes and found a long, club-like object.

Perliss was now at the top of the steps and he drew back the bolts. He delicately lifted the hatch and peered in.

"Oh, my friend," Red heard Oolah say. She had imagined him springing from behind the trap door to apprehend his jailers, but he must have been sitting on the bed all this time, probably feeling sorry for himself.

"Don't worry, I am here now," Perliss said, moving out of the hatch entrance. "I have tricked them. They will not hold my good friend any longer."

Red's eyes went wide, and she looked at Janna, who wore the same expression of horror.

"Oh, I knew someone like you would come to my rescue," Oolah said.

She gripped Janna's hand as they heard Oolah walk across the room. Then he was past Perliss and had one of his feet on the first of the steps.

"Wait until I get my hands upon those wretches," Oolah said.

Red backed away from the stairs, as did Janna. However, no sooner had they stepped away, had Oolah come tumbling down the steps. He fell quickly and landed in a heap on the floor. Perliss was shuffling after him as Red moved forward with her weapon held aloft.

"Do not touch him," Perliss said, brandishing his walking staff. "We must leave the scene looking natural," he added.

Red noticed the speckles of blood upon Perliss's walking cane and she realised what had happened.

Perliss came down the stairs and stood over Oolah as his weak looking eyes peered up in astonishment.

"Is it you that dares to hurt me?" Oolah said, his voice sounding aghast.

"I am far too late in the day," Perliss said. "But better late than never."

Oolah let out a cry as he saw Perliss lift the staff high, and then as he brought it down.

The next few moments were a blur. Perliss seemed to know exactly what he was doing. He told Red to scatter many objects from the boxes, and he himself placed one of the slim poles on a step. By the time they finished arranging things, the scene looked convincing.

"You, my angel, do not belong in a place like this. I feel that in my heart," Perliss said to Red.

"You are right. I am looking for my friend. I was in that shuttle crash."

Perliss looked at her with narrowing eyes. "The city has been talking about nothing else," he admitted. "There's much speculation about what happened to the crew."

"Well, you're looking at one of them," she said.

"You sustained no injuries?" he asked.

"Apart from a memory loss. But can you find my friend?"

Perliss shook his head. "Everyone is talking about it, but nobody knows what happened."

"Somebody knows," Red said, her eyes peering intently.

"I'm sure there must be someone. However, I do not mix in those circles. Tell me; what does your friend look like?"

Red thought for a moment and felt a little embarrassed. "I've lost my memory. I know the person is female. I can slightly picture her face and I think she's about the same age as I, but that is all."

"Then you make the task a difficult one."

"I would know her if I spotted her, especially in a city such as this," Red admitted.

Perliss nodded his head. "Then that is what you must do. I'm sorry that I can't be of more help."

Red nodded her head. He was a good man, and she sensed he would help her if he could, but this task was beyond him. It was probably beyond her, she thought. Going back into the city was her only option. She said as much to Perliss, but he did not seem keen.

"I can buy your passage out of here," he said. "Get to one of the other cities behind the desert and wait for your memory to return. Surely this young woman has parents that will want to investigate?"

A sudden flash of memory caught Red by surprise. She was in a tight, dark container, and they submerged her body in some kind of liquid. A feeling of suffocation gripped her.

"Are you alright?" Perliss asked, touching her arm.

Red shook her head and tried to replay what her mind had shown her. The memory remained a little while longer before fading to nothing. Maybe something Perliss had said triggered the recall. Maybe her mind would unlock more of her past, but the question was... did she really want to know?

Chapter Sixteen

Perliss had gone into the city. He gave instructions for the household to have strong alibis – not that the sentinel guards would want to interrogate them; they were just slaves, after all. When he returned, he seemed in high spirits.

"Here," he said to Red. "This is a bracelet that will gain you entrance to the city. It has a simple clasp, so you can take it off, but never do this where people can see."

Red took the bracelet and applied it to her wrist. "I thought you were against searching the city."

"I think you will search anyway," he said, which made Red smile. "I have also arranged transportation to Solar 1," he said. "It is the last of our cities. Then you can gain passage to Trillian, if you desire it. Find the blue gates and you'll find a transporter named

Vanda. I have given him instruction." Perlis passed her a credit disk. "Here, you'll need this. It has more than enough credits for you needs. Guard it well."

Red took the slim credit disk from Perrin's hand. "I don't know how to thank you," she said, but Perliss was already waving away her words.

"It is I that is indebted to you. I sensed Oolah was no good, but I had no way of proving it. You have not only aided me in this situation, but given me the means to take this household and make it good."

"And I'm sure that you will," Red smiled.

"Oh, and there's this," Perliss said, bringing out a cloak and holding it out to her. "It has a hood and is a common garment in the Solar districts. You will not stand out so much." Then he considered her. "But I would wear the hood up. Your face is far too delicate of features for these parts."

Again, Red thanked the man.

"You must leave now, because we must report the demise of our friend upstairs. And this place will soon teem with guards."

Red went to him and embraced him. Then he looked her in the eye. "Remember, the blue gates. That is where your passage will leave. Vanda will wear a headdress that wraps around the face. He is good, and he is discreet."

Red went to the others and embraced them. When she got to Janna and saw her tired, yet smiling face, she could not help but get emotional. They did not speak – the embrace was enough. Then Janna kissed Red's cheek.

"You have until the double sound of the gate alarms to search. If you are not at the gate in time, you will miss your ride. Good luck, my friend," Perliss said, as Red nodded and left the building.

· · • •• • • •• ·

It felt surreal walking away. The outside of the building was unfamiliar to her. She turned and looked up at the tower. Seeing the tiny window at the top made her feel uncomfortable. To think that she might still have been there, gazing out on a world that knew nothing of her plight, if she had not been able to draw in some inner strength, a strength she never would have admitted she possessed. Then she pictured her captor, lying dead on the next floor down, and her heart felt heavy with emotion. She told herself that from this horrid event, something good would blossom.

The building, despite its lack of love, could once again become beautiful. Red sighed and turned to face the last of the garden. Finding her crew member was paramount, and she did not have long.

She passed through two tall pillars that marked the boundary of Oolah's residence. The vegetation thinned until she was walking on bare sand. A moment later, she reached the gates of the city.

One of the city guards scanned her bracelet, and she moved along. A wave of heat greeted her. The noise was also a surprise after the solitude of her cell. Smells of street food and heavy perfume stalls filled her nostrils. She looked at the sprawling streets and the crowds of weaving people. Red did not know where to start.

Before she could think what to do next, she had to step aside as a couple of Fire maidens pushed past. The two ladies, clad in dark flowing clothing, with their eyes rimmed with smears of black, moved with purpose. They had bundles strapped to their back, which made a swishing sound. Their cargo, she surmised, must have been drinking containers. Red didn't know where they were going, but she guessed they were walking farther than the perimeter of the city. Still, the sight of the long strides and their flowing cloaks gave them an air of attitude, and even aggression.

She tried to think like an abductor. They could not keep their captive on the street for all to see.

Therefore, she needed to head towards the back streets. Dwellings and businesses were the best place to start. Perliss said that the credit disk had enough to bribe many people, but advised to offer a moderate amount; otherwise, she might bring too much attention.

The streets offered a brief respite from the humidity. People moved with little concern, but for their own passage. Beggars and sellers moved amongst the rich and the hopeless – just another day in the city, Red told herself.

She turned into a wider stretch and cut through the oncoming traffic. There were fewer traders here, at least not the kind offering street goods. Shops replaced market stalls. Darkly lit doorways gave sanctuary from the blazing sun. Exotic signs promoted wares that had not appeared for sale on the streets.

More Fire maidens passed, walking with purpose, their heads held high, their stance pompous as they cut through the crowds. She watched them go, cutting through the crowd like a sharp sword. For a moment, she wondered if something was about to happen. Maybe they had a calling, maybe a time of worship? Red was still contemplating the women when she glanced to her left.

A man was sitting down next to a small basket. He was a beggar. He had his credit machine held out before him, pleadingly.

"What is your language?" Red asked, squatting down beside him. The man shook his head and shoved the credit accumulator towards her. Red asked again, only in another language. Then the man nodded his head and spoke to her.

"I am an old man who cannot work," he said.

"Give me information and I'll pass you two credits."

The man shook his head. "But two credits will not buy much in such a harsh city."

"Very well. I will leave you to your day," she said, attempting to rise.

The man quickly put his bony hand on her arm and motioned her to stay.

"Make it three credits and I'll answer anything you want."

Red tapped at his screen, making the sum of the exchange, then inserted the disk, which spun once. Then she took it from the machine and the man nodded his head, happy with the transaction.

"There was a crash," Red said. "I want to know what happened to the people on-board."

The beggar nodded his head and smiled, displaying rotten teeth.

"Everyone is talking about the crash," he said, shrugging his shoulders. "People say that someone brought the craft down by using a pulse-charge."

"I am not interested in the ship or why it crashed. I want to know about the people."

"It is a mystery," the man said, smiling.

Red grabbed hold of his tunic. "I have paid you for information. If you don't know, then direct me to someone who does."

The man flinched; his arm came up to defend himself, as if he expected Red to strike. "They say a life-pod has been salvaged," he said. "There may have been someone inside. I know not where."

"If they brought a pod into the city, where would they hide it?"

"Ah," the man said, waving his finger. "You need the gadget district. If there really was a pod, they would soon have it off the street and stripped for parts."

Red eased her grip on the man's garment as he gave her directions. He told her to go to a drinking establishment called Dannit 4 and look for a person named Strin. If anyone knew about the pod, it would be her.

"She knows everything that happens in that area – she has eyes everywhere. You can't miss her. The woman is plump and dresses like a crazy lady. She always wears a flying hat. See that and you find her."

Feeling content with the information, Red stood up and promised to return if he was sending her on a fool's errand. The man reiterated that he was telling the truth. She thanked him and went on her way.

The streets got busier as Red crossed to the gadget district. The walkways were wider and the people frequenting this area changed. There were more men and more animals. Two agile looking people rode past on giant lizard-like creatures. These men sat on the crest of the animal's backs, which made them the same height as the second-story windows. They stopped to talk with a person who languished on a balcony. One man was making light with his chat while the other smiled at what he was saying. The woman seemed impressed and averted her eyes several times at just the right moment.

Red continued on and soon reached a junction. To her left stood one of the city gates. A sign stated that this was a yellow exit, and the doors coloured accordingly. The gates were open at that moment to let in a sand cruiser. This cruiser was towing a trailer, which also hovered a foot off the ground. However, the cargo had Red reeling.

Strapped to the loader was a hulking engine part and a large panel – the panel was from her ship. Like birds at an old carcass, the city vultures were picking apart the helpless craft. Red watched as one guard scanned a doc card and the sand cruiser moved forward. The gates closed after it, sealing out the golden dunes.

She joined the swell of the people. The cruiser came past her and she watched it pull its load along the main drag. Remembering the beggar's directions – "turn left when you reach an old disused well," Red let the cruiser pass from view and changed direction.

The road wound on. The old man had told her to look for a place called Dannit 4. Red was only half way along the strip when a shop entrance drew her attention. She felt compelled to enter.

The interior was bright and welcoming. Three men stood down an aisle, talking loudly. One of them held an object, turning it over in his hands. Red kept her distance.

The gadget warehouse held a little of everything. In the corner stood an engine cover, and beside it, various coiled objects. A small child's sand cruiser lay half-buried beneath other items.

"Can I help you?" a gaunt looking keeper asked, bowing his head, his hands clasped like a religious man.

"I will continue to look, if I may," Red replied, speaking in the same tongue as the man. Her ability to understand any language still baffled her, but no longer surprised her.

The salesperson nodded his head and left her browsing. Red walked around the interior, marvelling at the amount of variety. She was moving past several tall containers when she traced one of them with her finger. Red flinched and quickly removed her hand. Information flooded her head. For a moment, the sensory download made her quite dizzy. She stood there, waiting for the feeling to subside, which it did.

The object was a tall, square casket. She knew now that it was a container for a reactor-coil extractor. A picture formed and somehow she knew its age and colour. Red even knew how much the device was worth.

"That is a..." the salesperson began, but Red finished his sentence.

"It is a Mark 6 DDC extractor," she said.

The keeper's artificial smile faltered. "Why, yes," he said. "But what makes you say it's a Mark 6?"

Red looked at his face and then down at the container. She thought fast. "Oh, there are differences in the style of container – and a lucky guess," she said.

The man did not look entirely convinced, but he managed another smile. "You know your equipment, but I suspect that you have little need for reactor parts."

Red nodded. "I am looking for a life-pod. Have you any?"

The man stared at her for a moment, his sunken face giving away nothing. He looked her up and down, taking in her simple cloak.

Red needed to address his curiosity. "I ask for my master," she said. "He collects them.

The man bowed his head and seemed satisfied. "A strange object to collect," he said.

Red controlled her reply, sweeping the shop with her gaze as she spoke.

"I do not question his taste. I'm merely here to entertain his will."

"As you wish," the man said. "I do not have what you ask for."

"My master has received information that a pod has recently come onto the market."

The man looked flummoxed for a moment. His hands, still clasped, rubbed together. "I have not heard of such an item," he said. "Your master has been ill-informed. May I ask his name?"

Red ignored the question. She needed to move the conversation on.

"Well, if you don't have it, then one of the other – more comprehensive shops –may have it."

The man recoiled. "We are the largest stockist. We would have first refusal if a pod came to market."

Red, now content that the man was telling the truth, made ready to leave. As she moved away, she spotted a handheld device. She placed her palm on the smooth surface and smiled at her find.

"Ah," she said, picking up the item and inspecting it. She turned it over in her hand, feeling its weight, marvelling at its build quality. She could even picture the device's construction, and what machines constructed it. The rush of information about the object was fascinating. Her mind, now conditioned to receive this type of information, no longer caused her ill effects.

"Rare sonic cannon," the man said. "A short range blast, but one a person will remember."

"How much is it?" she asked.

"Fifty credits," the man said. "It is a fine example."

She shook her head. "It is only worth thirty," she said. "But I will offer you thirty-five."

The man looked insulted. "The price is fifty, but I'm willing to come down to forty-five."

"That is too much," she said, locking eyes with him. "The cartridge is half empty, and difficult to replenish. It has got little life left."

Red realised she should have inspected it before giving it such an in-depth critique.

"You could not know this," the man said, his brow furrowed.

Red composed herself, tossed the item into the air and caught it.

"I have owned one myself. And I can tell by its weight that it is half-empty. Maybe I will offer you thirty, not thirty-five."

The man looked at the object, eyeing it with suspicion. He was just a sales agent and probably had limited understanding of half the objects in the shop.

He smiled. "Again, you are well informed," he said. "But I remember you offering thirty-five?"

Red looked at the sonic cannon and then at the man. "We have a deal," she said, producing her credit disk from her pocket.

The man brought a credit collector to her, and she inserted the disk. As the machine was calculating, Red looked along the aisle. The three customers further down had stopped their conversation. They were watching her. One of them whispered to the others. Their expressions were hard, their gaze full of suspicion.

She slipped the weapon into her pocket and her disk into another. She exited the building, back to the sounds of the crowds and the harsh light. Red tried to control her breathing as she walked away. She turned her head and looked back. The salesperson was standing in the doorway with his collector still in hand. He was watching her and did not care if she knew.

Red looked ahead and noticed a distant sign up ahead saying, Dannit 4. She rushed forward, keen to be out of sight. When she looked back again, she saw the three men standing in the doorway. They looked at each other as the keeper spoke to them. Then they started forward, slowly, heading in the same direction.

Red turned away, cursing under her breath. "Well done," she whispered to herself. "Now you have men at your heels." She took a deep breath. Maybe she was being over dramatic, she thought. The men may have been ready to leave the shop, anyway.

Dannit 4 was closer now. Red chanced another glance over her shoulder. The three men were still advancing. All three of them were peering at her, their hard eyes not attempting to conceal their intent. As she approached Dannit 4, she made plans to lose them within the busy interior. Out of one situation and into another, she thought as she moved past people and headed for the entrance. The sooner she left this city, the better.

CHAPTER SEVENTEEN

The lift seemed deceptively slow as it slipped past floor after floor of the Syrin building. Manark watched the numbers change, the digits increasing as they climbed higher. The two security men that stood either side of him were unflinching in their posts.

"It's strange they have summoned me," he said, hoping to ignite a response. The men remained silent.

"Do you know the reason they want to see me?" he asked.

One man turned his head. "We do not have that information."

Manark nodded his head and looked down at his feet. He would learn nothing from these men. They simply followed orders and needed only minimal information to comply.

The counter continued to mark off the floors, and Manark hoped he was not going back to the same boardroom as before. But the lift stopped at thirty-nine. The doors opened, and they exited.

He walked down the corridor with the two men escorting him, their shoulders very close to his at all times. Then he spotted a person coming the other way. The same woman who had given him the eye in the park area looked at him, her dark pupils following his face.

Was that it, he thought? Surely, it was not a coincidence seeing the same woman. Maybe she was not an interaction droid after all, but an actual woman – and maybe his eyes had lingered on her for too long. Had she reported him for ogling her? Syrin, like most big corporations, took sexual harassment seriously.

The woman winked at him as she passed. What was that supposed to mean? Was she letting him know he was in for it, or was she, as he originally thought, just a flirtation-droid, programmed to boost men's egos within the company. He tried to calm his mind. It was just his imagination was getting the better of him.

The men stopped and pointed at a wide door. They were not joining him, much to Manark's relief. After the way they had marched him down the hall, he had visions of them following him into a space and beating him into a confession.

He entered the room and found himself before a wide desk set in front of picture windows. Behind the desk, a high-backed chair faced away, giving its occupant a view of the grounds below. The chair turned and Sarak looked at him with a small smile on her face.

"You wished to see me?" he said, feeling his pulse quicken. He would rather the two security men had attacked him.

"Sit," she said. Her voice was bitter, her nose wrinkling as she glanced down at a memo on her info-pad.

He took a seat and wondered just how much she knew. It was strange timing.

"Tell me what you've been doing?" she asked, her thick goggles rising to look at him.

He cleared his throat. Was she attempting to give him the chance to come clean, or hang himself? He could not tell.

"The data is quite extensive," he said. "It will take me some time to analyse."

"That moment has passed," she said, putting down her pad. "We need your findings now."

"But they are incomplete," he said, holding out his hands. He was relaxing now that she had not addressed his violation of the data code.

"Make a concerted guess from what you've seen."

He rubbed at one of his eyes with his finger. "This is no ordinary data," he said. "There are so many variables that it makes no sense right at this moment."

Sarak hit the desk with both hands, making him jump. "So, what are we paying you to do? This isn't a frigging library."

"I need more time," he said, and now he was sitting bolt straight. He would have to talk fast to gain ground with her.

"If you hadn't wasted your time reading private files, you might have more of an idea."

He felt a wave of trepidation and the veins in his neck pulsed. So she knew. How naïve was he to think otherwise?

"I was curious. Please forgive me."

Sarak looked at him with disdain. She got up from her desk, walked around it, and stood next to him. Being short, she did not have to stoop far to bring her face close to his.

"If I tell security about your override, they will take you. You will have no rights. You signed a disclaimer, remember." Sarak shifted her position and sat on the corner of the table, with her arms folded. "First, they will interrogate you about all you have seen, and then they will hold you until I set a trial. And believe me when I say this company donates quite a considerable sum to the city's legal department."

"You can't do that," Manark said, looking at her with pleading eyes.

"We can. And not only can we hold you, we can make sure you never work in this field again."

Manark's hands shook. He had hardly read the disclosures, but he reckoned they gave Syrin the power to do whatever they pleased in this situation. It took every bit of control not to reach across the desk and put his hands around her scrawny neck. Manark shook his head – he had been so foolish.

Sarak studied him for a moment, biting her bottom lip twice as if in contemplation. Then she wandered back to her chair.

"As head of this corporation, I have nobody above me. I answer only to the investors' committee," she said with a smile. "I have received a memo today calling for action. They say they can rectify our Arin problem." Sarak waved a hand, frivolously, in the air. "They seem to think they can catch the three runaways."

Manark looked down at her data pad. That memo arriving was the reason he was sitting here.

Sarak smiled and Manark knew that whatever followed would not be good. When she continued, her face was calm and collected – her chess move would be final, with no sign of a suitable counter attack.

"I'll let you into a secret," she said. "I've had enough of this Arin project. Some things are only good on paper. I want this thorn plucked from my side."

"How can I help you?" Manark asked.

Sarak tapped at her data pad and then pushed it across the table.

"I want you to read this. I had the legal department draw it up. It states that you categorically advise termination of all three AIs based upon your findings. You reason they are completely unstable and will resist any kind of reprograming." She sighed. "It has to look convincing."

Manark looked at the document on the screen and then at Sarak as she peered through her thick goggles.

"But this is untrue," he said. "Even if I tested the data, I don't think I could ever reach this conclusion."

"Well, you have today," she said, flashing a sneering smile. "Either you've reached this conclusion, or you've just violated your contract and possibly committed an act of sabotage, or even terrorist activity. The choice is yours."

Manark looked down once more at the data screen and then at Sarak's face.

Sarak drummed her fingers on the desk. "Sign it, god damn you!" she shouted.

He panted. He thought about what a trial could mean for him. Even if he got off, his name in this industry would be worthless. He would not find work. He gazed at her one last time and then signed the document and slid it towards her.

Sarak looked down at his signature. "Good," she said with a smile. "I'll give that to the committee. Thank you for your help with this matter," she said. "Your services are no longer required."

Manark stood up and walked away from the table on shaking legs. He felt as if he had just run five miles carrying a heavy weight. Then Sarak said one last thing to him, just as he reached the door.

"Don't let your conscience taint your mind. You have done the right thing. Have a good day, Manark."

Chapter Eighteen

The door to Dannit 4 opened and closed with a constant rhythm of customers. Red pushed through the crowds, stepped up onto the metal porch, and entered the establishment.

Huge ceiling-vents hummed loudly, delivering a much-needed freshness to the air. Neon signs and vid-screens lit the windowless interior. Promotions were everywhere. Some kind of music was playing. Vape machines on the far wall filled the air with strong, exotic scents. Several people were sucking on single vape-pipes, and in the corner was a collective pipe machine — a party of five were busy sharing their favourite flavour.

Red noticed a security monitor hanging above the bar. It reflected the entrance and a section of roadside. The crowd outside moved and shifted – and there stood her three stalkers beside a group of drinkers. Red watched them talk for a moment, and then one man disappeared from view, leaving the other two staring at the entrance. Red knew the other man was making his way down to the back of the building. His two friends mounted the metal platform, intent on entering.

A barman leaned over and asked her what she was having, but Red waved him away and left the bar. She decided it was time to move before her pursuers got inside and spotted her.

Red moved further into the long room, aiming for an archway along the back wall, content that the swell of people would hide her.

The room had a mix of people. Exotic looking merchants with colourful clothing laughed with each other, slapping each other on the back and swapping stories of sales lost and won. Tall, Tanakien street performers, with their yellow clothes decorated with their logo, keen to sooth their fevered brows, languished on tall stools, their juggling bars resting beside their feet. Day travellers stood out, with their goggles and sand hats still in place. With the greater percentage being mostly male, it was easy for her to search for the woman she needed.

The archway drew near, and she noticed a corridor. A short walk took her into a second room. It was just as busy as the first. Red approached a long bar near the back. She saw several drinks on offer, from blue Dallion liquids to Vallor shots, but the most expensive drink listed was water. At nearly three times the other beverages, it was an elitist drink, and the barman was never more careful than when he served this request.

The room was a bustle of moving bodies, but still she saw no signs of this elusive woman. Red checked to see if the men were following and found she was safe. She had a hand pushed deep into her pocket. The sonic cannon felt reassuring to her touch.

Only a single room remained. Had the beggar given her a bogus quest, she wondered? She thought not. He would not be so foolish.

She sighed and left the bar. Another corridor appeared, this one L-shaped. Beside the toilets stood more vape machines. Her eyes inspected each person she passed. Red moved with caution until she reached the last room. This one had a smaller bar, which served food. Great plates of steaming meats lay on trays, ready to reach eager mouths. She scanned the gathering, and her pulse quickened when she spotted the person she sought. The lady was plump, just as the beggar had said, and wearing an old flight hat, which looked out of place on her round, ruddy head.

Red slipped through a line of drinkers and rounded a couple of tables. She was heading over to the woman when a commotion near the exit caught her attention. A man was complaining as he tried to leave, but was quickly shoved aside by another man entering. A brief stand-off had everyone in the room waiting for a fight, then the one leaving backed down. Red recognised the man entering – one of her stalkers.

Red turned away, quickly took off her cloak, and draped it over her arm. She drifted towards the bar and slipped herself between two stout loaders who were taking a quick break. The shining vid screen displayed adverts for liquids. A barman slapped a metal drink-pad down in front of her and moved away.

The other side of the bar had a reflective plate, which mirrored the room behind her. She watched the reflection of the man as he stood in the centre of the room, inspecting the clientele. His head moved back and forth. The man's gaze happened her way and Red hunched over, resting her face in her hand, her fingers half concealing her face. The searching man continued to turn until he was facing away. Then he left the room and quickly disappeared down the far corridor.

A voice asked her what she wanted. It was a droid, and not an expensive one. The robot waited, its overtly synthetic face looking at her. The machine blinked once and tilted its head.

Red pointed at a drink and produced her disk, which the robot took and scanned. Then a slim cylindrical container appeared before her. When he passed her the disk, their fingers connected and reams of information rushed into her mind. She now knew that the droid was a TR 47, second-generation model. The robot was the first to have fully articulated lips to mimic actual speech and hide the fitted sound coil. She knew the names of his previous owners – and even when Dannit 4 had purchased him.

The robot stared at her for a moment, as if confused, and Red wondered if he could sense the information leaving his cells. Red quickly nodded and took the drink and turned.

All thoughts about the droid quickly vanished when she realised the woman with the flight hat had gone. An inner panic rippled through her body. Behind the bar, the clock counted out the seconds, and she thought about her ride leaving without her. Red looked about and went to where the woman had been sitting. Two elderly men with skin like dried mud sat laughing. Red asked them where the person with the hat had gone. They looked at each other and then one of them pointed towards the exit.

The heat hit her, blinding her eyes and caressing her delicate skin. Red put on her cloak and pulled her hood up over her head. The back of the property was sparse, and she could not see the woman anywhere. Two people walked past her, and then a third. The sight of this last person made Red's breathing quicken.

She only saw Jar from behind, but he was unmistakable. He strode off with a bottle in hand. His swagger was carefree, and he was humming some unheard tune.

Red pulled her hood down further and took a long drink from her tube. She grimaced at the taste, but she needed courage. She took another drink, then another, and slapped the empty container down on one of the outside tables. Then she walked.

The street beyond was traffic free. The area largely comprised retail buildings and market stalls. She kept pace with Jar, her eyes not leaving him even for one second. He knew nothing of her presence; she was sure of that.

Jar waved at several people that he knew, once or twice shouting something with that beefy voice of his. When he stopped walking, she waited. He slowly slipped his hand under a canopy and quietly produced a piece of fruit. Then he was on his way again, quickly devouring the free snack while he ambled along. Jar glanced to his left and eyed a passing woman. He said something to her, trying his luck, but the woman kept walking. A moment later, he cursed at two passing Fire maidens. Their pale faces did not falter as Jar shouted vile things in their direction. He even spat as they passed.

Red followed Jar into a narrow street. This marked the end of the market stalls. Boxes and discarded waste littered the back of the shops. Then, half way down, Jar stopped and turned.

"You had better have a good reason for following me," he said as he came striding back towards her.

Red watched from the darkness of her hood. She waited until he was closer. Her inner anger found a new level as she peered at his round, stupid face. She glanced about. The back alley was devoid of people – at least for the moment. He came forward, confident that the small person before him was no threat.

She lifted both her hands and flipped back her hood, revealing her scowling face.

Jar was only ten paces away from her, and the sight of her made him stop dead in his tracks.

"This cannot be," he said, his mind working hard to comprehend. "But where is Oolah?" he said, expecting to see the man close by. He even looked round, as if the man were playing some kind of silly hoax.

"I am alone," Red replied. "Oolah is dead."

She saw Jar shake his head. "You lie." Then he realised she was talking to him in his own language and not Majarri. "Who are you?" he said, his eyes considering her.

Red slid the hand cannon from her pocket. "I am the one who will kill you if you move."

"Wow," Jar said, holding his hands up. "That is no toy that you hold. You do not know its power."

"This," Red said, as if inspecting it. "You mean the cannon that I'm holding?" Then she listed its schematics and even its serial codes. "At least you recognise the fact that I can kill you with one twitch of my finger."

"You are not as you look," Jar said, looking a little frightened. "How did you escape, Oolah?"

"He died in the same way you will," she said, lifting the cannon to point at his face.

"Wait," he said, waving his hands. A bead of sweat ran down his face – he forced a smile. "If you wanted me dead, you would have done so already. But something tells me you want something from good-old Jar."

"Believe me when I say there is nothing I want from you. I will do Solar 3 a favour."

"Please," he said. "Ask what you want and it will be yours."

"Tell me this," she began. "Did you take the life pod?"

"I know nothing about... did you say a pod?"

Red shook her head and re-aimed the cannon.

"No, please. Wait. I have information."

Red lowered the gun a little and waited.

"They took the person in the pod. And if the pod came with her, I don't know who has it now."

"And the person within?" she asked.

"I know nothing of a person within..."

Red lifted the cannon a third time and suddenly the large man's memory recalled more details.

"Your friend is no longer here," he said, his breath short and his voice quick. "They smuggled her out on a caravan. Five, maybe six large wagons heading for Solar 2, I think. She is in one of those wagons. A future slave maybe, but she is alive. They would not dare kill a..." he paused for a moment, trying to find the right words, "she is a good commodity."

"As were I," Red said through clasped teeth.

Jar held his hands out in mock surrender. "Please be merciful," he pleaded. "It is harsh, this city. I do what I do to survive."

"Even if that means selling people into a private hell?"

"I can help you find your friend," he said, and then suddenly he was making a desperate dash for her.

Red was quick. She side stepped and let the cannon fire. Jar fell forward, clutching his wrist as he fell. His hand had vanished, leaving only a smouldering stump.

He rolled around on the floor, still squeezing his wrist.

"Don't worry – I set it for short blasts. You do not need to hold the wrist. The cannon uses concentrated light. It would have sealed your wound." As if to satisfy her curiosity, she leaned over him to see that all she said was correct. "It's clean, but I will now reset the device to do more damage – a sonic blast, maybe."

Jar made to move, but Red quickly tutted and held the cannon just inches from his face.

"What do you want?" Jar shouted – his face a mask of pain – his forehead wet with perspiration.

"I have all that I need," she said. "You are free to go, but know this. I came here to investigate you. We are everywhere. You are being watched."

Jar looked about, squinting. His eyes searched the tops of the buildings and the shady doors below. He remained silent, as if he was trying to decide whether she was telling the truth.

"If you don't believe me, ask yourself why I am standing here and why Oolah is dead in his tower. You will soon hear of an accident. We have cleaned up the situation. Now I must leave, but know this... we are strong and we are many. If I hear you are planning revenge, you will die."

Jar shook his head, and Red felt very pleased with her subterfuge. She noted his expression, the tightness of his mouth, the recognition in his gaze – the man was now convinced. Red smiled. As hard as it was to admit, she liked this feeling. He looked about, scanning the buildings. That she stood before him was enough to convince him of her words.

"I will go now. I was never here. Remember, we are strong."

Red put the cannon back into her pocket. She stared at him for a moment longer. "I guess your fruit swiping days are over," she said, as she turned and walked away.

"I will be a good man," he shouted after her. He was kneeling now, his face still a mask of pain. He looked at his handless wrist and then shouted again, this time looking about, as if people were watching him. "I swear I will be a good man."

Red found another passageway and, once she was out of Jar's line of sight, she ran with all her might. Her hands were trembling. She could not believe how bold she had been. The swarms of people ignited her senses. Her prize was that she now knew where her friend was. All she had to do now was get to the right portal in time, and convince her lift to help her find this missing crewmember.

Chapter Nineteen

R ed sat drumming her fingers on a table. The outdoor food vender was a cheap and busy place. With nothing more than to replenish her energies, she had eaten a meal. Then she sat watching a clock that hung from a central pillar that supported a billowing canopy and waited.

The dominant sun was slipping towards the horizon. A second, less powerful sun was working its way into the sky, bringing this area of the planet into a semi-gloom. Soon the shadows would come crawling and tower lighting would sparkle into life.

Red looked around at the boisterous drinkers and marvelled at the variety. How they came to be here she did not know, because not all of them looked Solar born, or travelling through. She guessed that some had arrived here and rested a little too long.

This was the place for complacency. They languished like scavengers on a rock, content to eke out their existence with little fuss. The more that she looked, the more that she knew her journey lay elsewhere.

She looked over at the city clock and checked the passage of time. Her shipmate was alone and frightened, possibly shackled in the back of a hot, dusty wagon. Time was of the essence if she was going to catch up. A long caravan meant she had a good chance of closing the gap. Red hoped she was not too late.

A blinding flash of memory came to mind. She gripped the table as the image jolted her. She pictured White. Yes, that was her name – her name a colour, just like her own – the girl looked just a year or two younger. Her face was just as pale and fresh.

The memory was confusing. White was reaching out to her with her hand. At first, Red thought the girl was crying profusely, but she quickly realised that the droplets on her face were not tears, but some kind of liquid. Then someone was pulling her away. Red reached out, but it was no good. Whatever shackles held her, prevented her from grabbing hold.

She noticed a growing silence as the drinking establishment came back into focus. The people sitting closest were all staring at her. They swapped glances. Red noticed a barman as he shuffled over to a tall man wiping a counter with a filthy rag. They whispered together.

Red finished her drink and stood up. She had overstayed her welcome. It was time to visit the city exit.

The gates were a hive of activity. Several wheeled-carts lined up amongst the hover-cruisers and hover bikes. Crowds of people shifted and shoved to board or exit by other means. Two men were checking the papers of a four cart caravan. Behind this procession lay Red's ride.

The owner of the wagon was a tall, slightly gaunt man with skin the colour of the desert dunes. Here was a man that was surely Solar born. He covered his head with carefully wrapped material. His face scarf hung loose, exposing a stubbly chin. He looked every bit the hardened traveller.

"Hello," Red said, striding up to him. "You must be Vanda." The man did not speak, but beckoned her with one bony hand. They went around the back of his cart and he told her to check the securing straps.

Red did as he asked. She thought it odd that they had not exchanged pleasantries, but then she quickly discovered the reason.

A man with a digit-tablet came walking along. He was peering at the screen and then at both of them.

"I have no listing for two people," he said. "One cart, one driver, luggage, gadget parts and plasma tubes."

"No, no," the driver said. "One driver, one loader."

"The guard looked at Red as she continued to secure the bundle in place.

"This happened last week," the driver said. "How many times can the Watchers get this wrong?"

"I'm going to have to check," the guard said.

"I'm heading for Solar One," the driver argued, his exasperation etched upon his time-lined face. "If I'm delayed, I will have to travel through the night storms. Do not do this to me."

The guard stooped to look under Red's hood – she looked him in the eye and smiled. He gave a huff of dissatisfaction as he tapped his pad, amending the info.

The driver told her to get in the front. Red walked along the cart, which was sizable. The cargo, which another attendant was busy checking, lay covered with strong grey skins and secured by rope.

She climbed up into the cab. Four carbon poles supported a simply made canopy, which rippled with the breeze. This covering was makeshift, but worked well as a barrier against the harsh sun. The chair was comfortable, and there, on the foot well, was a box of sweet smelling fruits.

The man climbed aboard, took up the reins, and remained silent. He did not look at Red. The twin beasts that pulled the cart glanced back, sniffing the air. Red smiled at them and hoped they were friendly.

"We will speak once we are beyond the gate," the driver whispered as the caravan in front started away.

The guard came alongside the driver and swiped his data pad, giving them electronic permission to leave.

"The next time this happens, I will have to check, so do yourself a favour and have yourself in order," the guard said, giving Red another glance.

They sat watching as the last of the caravan disappeared into the early evening, its rickety carriages shifting and rocking as it ground its way across the compressed desert sands. A noise had Red turning her head, and she saw a sand cruiser pass. It quickly navigated the caravan and then sped off, disturbing the floor and sending a cloud of dust into the air.

A gate guard flagged them forward. The driver gave one swift tug of the reins and the beasts started away. Once moving, the driver tied the reins to a post that jutted up from his platform and he relaxed back.

"Aren't you going to steer?" Red asked.

"They know the way. There is only one junction and I do not need to lead them until then. They are good Bollaboo."

"Bollaboo. That is a pleasant name," Red said, and smiled.

"They are a friendly beast, and always happy to do whatever I ask. And always on the lookout for a sweet treat," the driver said, reaching down and taking out two pieces of fruit and throwing the gifts towards them. Both the animals turned their slender necks, caught the tasty food in their jaws, and munched contentedly.

The driver suddenly put out his hand. "As you know, I am Vanda," he said. Red shook his rough hand and announced her own name. She turned and took one last look at the vast city wall. In the gloom, she thought she spotted the remains of her downed craft, but maybe it was a trick of the light across the dunes.

"You do not care for my city," Vanda said.

"I don't think I saw the best of it," Red responded, which made the man chuckle.

"It can be a harsh place. Many people with many problems."

"But you've probably lived here all your life."

"That is true. As soon as I was old enough, I dispatched goods. I am away for half the year. It keeps me sane."

"Did Perliss explain my situation?"

"He did," the driver said.

"Then you know what happened to me?"

"I do, and I am deeply sorry."

"What you don't know, is that I've got even with the man that kidnapped me."

"You kill him?" Vanda asked, casually.

"No. But I gave him something to think about."

"Do I know this man?"

"I know him as Jar."

"Ah," the man said. "You have done what many have thought of doing. He is a heathen. He takes what he sees. I have lost cargo to this man." Vanda patted her shoulder. "I am in your debt if you have punished him."

Red was still looking towards the horizon. "I did it for myself and I did it for all the poor unfortunates that have passed through the gates and fell foul to his dealings."

Vanda turned his head towards her. "Then the city should pin a badge on you." He broke into a laugh and Red laughed, too. A short moment ago, the thought of laughing seemed like an alien thing. Maybe it was the changing light on the land, or the gentle rocking of the carriage... or maybe it was the fast disappearing city wall. Whatever it was, it felt good to smile.

Chapter Twenty

T he sand beneath their wheels crunched and moved, making their cart dip and sway. Behind them, the trailers that they pulled followed the same line, rolling and swaying, and now Red knew why they had spent some time securing their cargo with a firm covering and guide ropes.

Up ahead, caravan that they were following suddenly deviated, moving off to the left, their hefty carriages cutting a deeper rut in through the sand. A tall sleeping-car hid from view the drivers up ahead, and the beasts that heaved the caravan.

"Are we not going the same way?"

"They are heading for a small outpost," the driver replied.

"I need a favour from you," Red said.

"Ask away."

"There's another caravan some way ahead. They left in the night. Is it possible to catch them?"

Vanda rubbed his chin. "Yes, I would say that it is possible. But how quickly will depend on how many trailers they tow and what cargo?"

Red nodded her head. "There are four, five or even six trailers, or so I was told."

"Then we may have a chance," he said. "Caravans are lazy. They amble along and love to make camp. They eat and sleep more than they travel. Not like transporters."

"Even if they have a hostage?" she asked.

Vanda looked at her, his eyes narrowing. "A hostage, you say. Is that true?"

"Yes, a girl, just like me, only younger."

The man studied her face for a moment, and Red could see that he was thinking.

"As you can see, I am no warrior, but I cannot go about my business knowing what I know. Caravan owners are not good people. We have to save the girl."

Red looked at Vanda and saw something in his eyes, deep conviction giving them life. She was both grateful and uncomfortable that such a man wanted to help. Yes, he was no fighter, but at that moment, sitting on Vanda's wagon, with nothing but the vastness of the desert land, she had to take what she could and hope for the best. She just hoped that she hadn't pulled the man into a danger far beyond their capabilities, whatever they were.

Vanda untied the reins and gave a sizable flick. The beasts in front suddenly sprinted, jerking the wagon forward. They threw red about, whereas Vanda, with all his years of experience, lifted himself from his seat and rode out the sudden movement.

"Can they run for long?" she asked.

"If I urged them, they would run all the way to Solar One. Of course I will not do that, but now and again we will push forward."

Red felt her heart lift in spirit. Soon, they were travelling at speed. The cart rocked, and the wheels made a swishing sound as they travelled. Red imagined meeting with the caravan crew, and her hand absently reached into her pocket, gripping her sonic cannon.

The light was changing as the second sun came higher in the sky and the more aggressive one drifted below the horizon. Red leaned her head against one of the carbon poles and wondered how she could disarm the caravan guards before they had time to grab White. Before long, the gentle rocking of the cab subdued her over productive mind and her lids closed. Then she slept.

• • • • • • • • • •

Red woke with a start. Her heart was beating fast. She looked around and saw Vanda's smiling face.

"Welcome back," he said.

Red remembered her dream, as if a dream it was. It involved a machine. They tied her down. A woman leaned over her. A man was speaking, using various terms that Red did not understand. She detected sensed something about the woman that she did not like; something intrinsically sour. She was not very tall and her face looked pinched. Two small eyes considered Red through her thick vis-goggles. Then the woman nodded her head. Red felt a burning pain and cried out.

"You have been asleep for a while," Vanda said.

Looking about, Red could tell that they had been travelling for some time. The sky was now crimson. The desert, though still lit enough to navigate, was a mass of shapes and shadows. A cool wind blew from the east, soothing her heated skin.

"Here, eat something," the driver said.

She took a cube of meat from his styrene container. It was strange how the occupants of Solar 3 favoured authentic foods instead of synthetic pastes. "What is it?" she asked.

"You don't want to know," Vanda said, taking a cube for himself, and then sitting back. "It's very nutritional. That's all you need to know.

Red looked at her meat again. Even her unusual ability to learn things from touch could not fathom what it was. She guessed it was various animals all pulped together. However, since Vanda was not about to bring out a nutrition tube, she had little choice.

"Who is Blue?" Vanda asked.

Red looked at the driver and thought for a moment. "I don't know."

"You said, Blue - I need to see Blue. I think that's what woke you."

Red said the name over in her mind, but nothing happened. She remembered White and could even picture her face now, but Blue was a new name. Then she looked at the two beasts out in front.

"You've slowed them."

"They were at full speed for quite a while. I thought they could do with a rest. I will sprint them again soon.

A silence followed and the vast desert whispered to them. The cool breeze carried drifts of sand from the mountainous dunes. The deep magenta burned and coated everything with its vivid magic.

"Is it always this beautiful?" Red asked, breaking the silence.

"It's the only time I truly feel alive," Vanda said, and seemed pleased that he was sitting with someone who could appreciate its quality. "But I think there might be a sand storm later – then you will see another side to this land. So what's your story?" he asked, changing the subject.

"I don't know," Red replied. "I have no memory of my past."

"That may be a good thing," he said.

"Maybe. But I know that the person I seek, somewhere out there, is a link to that past."

"You say she is a prisoner?"

"Yes. And I intend to rectify that situation."

"Is that why you're carrying that weapon?"

Red faltered. Her hand went instinctively to her pocket.

"Don't worry, I haven't taken it," Vanda said. "You were reclining, and it was protruding from your pocket. I couldn't help but notice it."

She nodded her head and felt a little ashamed that she should have such an item in her possession.

"I was alone in that city and several people were after me. I needed protection."

"Oh, I'm not criticising. Solar cities are not for the single person. You did well to gain it. I have a weapon under my seat, in case sand pirates make a visit."

Red felt a little easier at hearing his confession. "So what's your story?" she asked.

"Nothing much to tell. I was born to a wonderful mother and father and I followed in his trade."

"No wife or children?" Red asked.

Vanda did not speak for a moment.

"My wife turned to religion. She became a fire maiden. She worships the cycles of the suns."

"Are those the ladies with the flames painted on their foreheads?" Red asked.

"That is the ones. I knew her interest in that religion when I met her, but never thought it would consume her so."

"Why is it so bad to become a fire maiden?"

"They brainwash a person and make them abandon every aspect of their past life, possessions, friends, family, loved ones."

"Maybe one day she will abandon her beliefs and reunite with you."

"She had better hurry," Vanda said. "When a fire maiden turns fifty, she must sacrifice herself to the flame."

Red gasped and stared at Vanda in disbelief.

"She will simply walk into the flames and be no more," Vanda admitted.

"That cannot be legal – people can't just take their life in the name of religion."

"Each full year they talk about making it illegal, but nothing gets done."

Vanda seized up the reins again and gave them a quick snap, which stirred the beasts into action. "Time to get moving," he said, ending the conversation.

The cart rocked more frequently and the desert breeze seemed to increase. A heavenly coolness refreshed her face and neck. She wished she were alone at that moment to take off her clothing and enjoy the feeling.

"You can remove that heavy cloak, if you like," Vanda said, as if reading her thoughts.

She smiled at Vanda. He was a good man, and she was so lucky with her ride.

She pondered removing the garment when the front of the cart suddenly rose precariously as they mounted a large dune. The animals panted as they heaved the cargo up the bank of sand, which must have been at least thirty feet in height.

Finally, they reached the top and Red marvelled at the view. The desert stretched out before them, a carpet of gold that almost sparkled. Vanda pulled them to a stop before they descended.

"What is it?" Red asked, peering into the gloom.

Vanda looked at her and then pointed ahead. "There," he said.

She followed his pointing hand, but could see nothing.

"Look on the horizon," he said. "There is a speck of light. Nothing more than a glint, but it is there."

Red scrutinised the horizon line and, after a moment, spotted what she took to be a tiny star.

"What is it?" she asked.

"That is a tail light of a cart," he said.

Red felt her breath catch in her throat. "Is it a caravan?"

Vanda reached behind his seat and brought out a pair of vision gainers. He held them up to his eyes and held down a switch. The device hummed as it zeroed in on the object.

"It looks like a caravan," he said. "I can't make out how long the vehicle is, but that cart looks like a sleeping compartment, which is often a feature of a long caravan."

"Let me see," Red said.

Vanda passed her the gainers and Red studied the scene ahead. He was right. The carriage was wide, with a tiny window fitted central to its rounded swell.

"How did you notice that from here?" she asked.

"I have spent my life on these plains. Robbery is common here. You get to spot things that should not be there," he said.

Red studied the swaying cart for a moment longer before passing the vision gainers back.

"Do you think it's the caravan I'm seeking?" she asked.

"I was waiting in the queue all afternoon, waiting, because I like to leave ahead of the rest. There was no caravan longer than four carriages, so this one must have left at the time you were told."

"Can we sneak up on them?" she asked.

Vanda smiled. "What do you think?"

Chapter Twenty-One

T he board meeting started in one of the larger labs, deep within Syrin's vast underground bunker. This area, reserved for demonstrations to keep the investors informed, was a hive of conversation.

"This is most unacceptable," Acrin said, his thick, platted beard twitching with every word he uttered.

Sarak looked at him and carefully adjusted her goggles. She had no time for this man. In fact, she detested him. If it were not for his thirty percent share of investments, she would have ditched him a long time ago – and she meant this in a literal sense.

"We can only give you information as we collate it," Sarak said.

"But we were told that the ship malfunctioned, which I found to be most irregular. Then –"

"We make AIs and droids, not shuttles," Sarak said. "And the data originally pointed to a malfunction, but now we know different."

"So, which is the truth?" a middle-aged woman asked. She had not been privy to some correspondence because, with only a two percent share of investment, she could not access Class A documents.

Acrin turned to the woman. "Now they say that our AIs sabotaged their mission."

Sarak sighed. She hated when anyone used the word, *Our...*

"The initial intel suggested a system breakdown. It wasn't until we discovered the crash that we realised it was no longer a rescue situation."

"Not a rescue?" a Chinese investor said, leaning forward.

"You told us the AIs were unharmed?" Acrin furthered.

"What we told you was that their life signs were still functioning," Sarak corrected. "We based our assessment on data at the time of the crash – after the ship died, so did the readings."

Again murmurs came from the gathered people.

"The crash was no accident," Sarak emphasised. "The male crew-member sabotaged the ship. We have found evidence to support this. He disabled several coolant tanks and mixed them with fuel to combust the hull."

"Would he do this, knowing it could kill him?" the Chinese investor asked.

Sarak looked at her chief investor, Davan, who stood up. Davan typed a serial code on his datapad, and each pad around the board flashed in recognition.

"This is a document written by Dr Manark," Davan began. "Manark, as most of you will know, designed the memory instalments. You can read the report at your leisure, but let me assure you his findings are quite conclusive."

"Thank you, Davan," Sarak said. "He has found a deep contamination within all three AIs. These contaminations, based upon bio readings at the time of the crash, suggest that their neural networks are irreparable."

"He suggests this, or is it fact?" Acrin asked.

Sarak paused sufficiently before replying. "I'm afraid it is a fact."

Murmurs passed around the gathered committee. The Chinese man turned to his partner and conferred. Acrin turned to look at the woman opposite, who had the same look of unease.

"You guaranteed that this could not happen," Acrin said, looking at Sarak.

"Oh, come on," Sarak said, leaning on the table. "You know that with science, there is no absolute. Nature has a way of fucking it all up, no matter how much work we put in."

"It's outrageous," Acrin said, his fingers drumming on the polished surface of the desk.

"So what exactly *have* we invested in?" the Chinese man asked.

Sarak stood up. "What your credits have achieved is five years of research. We can sell that research on at ten times what you have given. A tidy return," she said, brandishing a cool smile.

"You said that our investments would reap twice that," Acrin said.

"An investment with high returns always runs risks," Davan said, holding his hands out before him. "But this is still a victory, is it not?"

"Is there no way to retrieve these AIs?" the woman asked.

Sarak was shaking her head. "I've issued a total lock down on all future production – excluding droids, of course. There are too many anomalies. We need to test what we have and learn from it. The document you have before you will leave no doubt what we must do."

"So how will you destroy these rogue AIs?" the Chinese man asked.

"Well, it's interesting that you should ask," Sarak replied, a rare, genuine smile challenging her tiny mouth.

Sarak turned, nodded her head, and Davan tapped his pad again.

"As you know, we have three major phases in place," Sarak continued. "We have our More than Real droid production, and we have our tech developments. Let me now show you something that we are working on for the private sector, and possible military use."

Behind Sarak, two enormous steel doors parted, revealing a larger lab. Workbenches lined each wall, and a circular stage occupied the centre. Various scientists were in the lab, going about their business as if the investors were not present. Structural equipment moved and pulsed like some old-school horror experiment, some of which sent static bursts high into the air.

"Let us introduce our latest project," Sarak said.

A door on the right slid open and something walked out. It was grey. The only clothing it wore was to cover its genitals. Its torso and limbs were human, but its four fingered hands and large, lizard like head reminded the committee that it was anything but.

The investors watched as the creature mounted the stage.

Acrin gazed, open-mouthed. The woman opposite could not hold the animal's gaze as its large reptilian eyes considered her. The two Chinese men stared motionless, and Sarak knew the image of the beast had hypnotised them. She could almost see their minds assessing how many shares they might gain.

"Impressive, isn't he?" she said, turning briefly to look at the creation. "We only have a code name for him at the moment, but I like to refer to him as The Raptor."

"Is there any dinosaur in him?" Acrin asked, his voice sounding astonished by what he was seeing.

Sarak shook her head. "No. The colonisers only brought one strand of dinosaur codes to this planet – we used a fine mix of various reptilian DNA. Of course, I am not at liberty to say more on that subject."

"Is he for sale?" one of the Chinese men asked.

"Not completely," Sarak replied, tilting her head. "But we are ready for share bidding."

"Oh, so this is the real reason that we are here – this is just another credit hunt," Acrin said with a shake of his head. "I thought we were going to talk about solutions, but I see this is just another marketing campaign."

Sarak looked at the man. God, how she hated him. Her nickname for him was Acrid, and she fought the temptation to use the name. It would be a shame if the product behind her should ever find this man in a darker, more secluded part of the building. Who knew what mistakes could happen?

"We are showing you our solution. As a bonus, you will be the first to have shares before outside investors have a chance."

"He looks impressive, but what can he do?" the investor asked. "I mean, from what you tell me, our rogue AIs have some pretty amazing qualities."

Sarak did not reply. She turned and addressed the workers in the lab. "Start an attack program. Number seven will be... entertaining, I think."

Hearing the announcement, the lizard-man flexed his muscles and preceded to ready himself for whatever happened next. His arms pulsed and tendons twitched. He jumped high in the air and back-flipped. Then he stood on his hands and, in one swift movement, lifted his entire weight with just two fingers.

"He loves his warm-ups," Sarak said casually, gazing at the investors through her thick goggles. "Please observe carefully. We have over twenty of our micro-bots of varying designs – and they are all programmed to kill our Raptor man."

Three bots clambered across the grid of pipework above the lab floor. They were small, the size of large cats, and covered in hair. They were quick, too. One of them leapt at the lizard, aiming for its head. The creature, however, was more agile. He dodged and grabbed hold of the insignificant bot and broke it in half before discarding it. The pieces lay at his feet amid an arc of hydraulic fluid and mechanisms.

A second cat-like bot launched, as did a third. The Raptor man, as Sarak had named him, dived back, flipping repeatedly. One of the small furry bots met with the beast's foot and it sailed up into the air, hitting the ceiling with speed. A third bot reached him and sank its metal teeth deep into the creature's leg. The lizard man grabbed the thing with both hands, pulled it away, and bit into its hard body. The helpless robotics splintered, and the bot died.

A frenzy of activity followed as the remaining droids came at once. They hit from all angles. Reaching down, the Raptor man took an object from a pouch and activated what looked like a luminous piece of string, which suddenly went taught. Using the object like a flexible staff, the Beast slashed through its attackers with ease. The lizard-man pinned down one bot with its four-toed foot and squeezed the thing to a pulp while punching away another. Again, the beast's speed was incredible.

Sarak did not watch. She had seen this test many times. She did not like the amount of waste, bot wise, but investors needed to feel confident. An excellent demonstration was far better than anything the firm could voice.

Five bots remained and the lizard-man had only sustained three injuries – and only one of these was deep enough for concern. The creature let out a huge cry of anger and went into overdrive, sweeping its cane in every direction as it closed in on its foes.

The investors sat watching. Sarak studied their faces. Stupid people, she thought, sitting there with their moronic expressions, watching the display like children watching a light show. It was a good thing they had sizable credits. Soon, Syrin would not need the likes of these pathetic individuals. Soon they would be self-funding and operate as the largest organic tech providers.

Sarak turned once the noise died down. The Raptor man was standing alone amid a carpet of broken biomechanics. He was panting and his lime green eyes were alive with energy. The animal liked the feeling of victory, as did Sarak. Her expression was one of admiration.

When Sarak turned, one of the Chinese men had taken out his personal silver-plated data pad. "How much do you need?" he asked.

Sarak walked towards the two men, but paused beside the woman shareholder. "Has that demonstration answered your question?"

The woman gazed at the lizard like thing with an unflinching gaze. "I pity the AIs when they meet it."

Sarak took a last look back at the beast. "I think those three AIs won't have a hope in hell."

Chapter Twenty-Two

T hey waited, poised at the top of the dune. That tiny pinpoint of light was still bouncing in the distance.

"How do you want to tackle this?" she asked Vanda.

The driver considered the question. "They could have guards watching the land," he said, rubbing his chin. "But they are lazy people – and they like the blue liquid – so let's hope they are making merry. There is one area, however, that is blind, and that is the very end of the caravan."

"If they don't spot us before we reach the back."

"A chance we will have to take – it is our only line of attack," he said.

Red did not like the use of the word attack. "I do not want to be so... gung-ho," she said. "I want to take the caravan bit by bit, without bloodshed, if possible."

"That is wise," Vanda said, nodding his head. "But I would bet that your friend is being held in that last carriage. And if that is the case, then we might get lucky and disappear back into the night without fuss."

"I really hope so," Red said with a smile.

With one swift crack of the reins, they were off, and with the steep dip of the land, they were soon making good speed.

Red tried to control her breathing. She focused on the pinprick of light and hoped they were not too late for her friend.

The land levelled out and their speed increased. Many passing caravans had compressed the sand, helping the wheels to turn smoothly and without drag. Lowering their heads, the two animals found the scent of the wagons ahead. They made small joyous murmurs as they raced towards their goal.

The caravan was travelling slowly. What had been a minor star of light was now recognisable as an energy crystal. It rocked from side to side in its housing, as if it was trying to hypnotise them.

Vanda slowed the animals so that their feet did not send up clouds of sand.

Red could now see a single porthole in the last car of the caravan. No illumination came from the carriage, which meant that the window had shutters.

"Do not worry," Vanda whispered, noting the look on her face. "We may be lucky. Yes, they could have guards, but these travellers like to sit together, near the front. They usually have one eye on the road and one on the cork.

They drew closer still to the shifting caravan. Red heard distant laughter as the group of caravan drivers taunted each other and swapped tales. She could smell boiling food and now and again, someone would curse and belch in equal measures. This was good – this would help cover any noise they made in their approach.

She focussed on the back of the wagon. The energy crystal swayed like a drunk. It illuminated a single door, and a fixed step. Red did not want to find a guard keeping watch in the sleeping car.

Vanda reined in his animals until they matched the speed of the carriage ahead. Red noted his sharp eyes peering intently. With a sigh of displeasure, Vanda shook his head. Red frowned as she tried to understand what was puzzling him so. Then she saw him gesture at the roof of the last carriage.

A man, heavily clothed in white rags, came carefully along a narrow running plate that spanned the length of the cart. His head was down, and in his drunken state, he was more interested in the placing of his feet than in looking out at his surroundings.

Red's heart fluttered. If this man glanced back now, he would surely discover them. She put her hand into her pocket and felt the metallic surface of her cannon.

The man stopped and leaned back while holding on to a roof handle. He slid open a hatch and reached inside with his free hand. His hand retracted, clutching a pottery jug. Evidently, their liquid was running low. He pushed back the hatch door, fastened it, and readied for his return journey.

"That was horrible," Red said once the man was out of view. "We were lucky."

"We have our advantage," Vanda said. "This man coming to retrieve more drink, in their eyes, will make up an inspection. They believe themselves safe. This is our window of opportunity."

Red nodded her head.

Vanda gave a gentle tap of the reins and the creatures out in front drifted a little closer to the cart.

"How do we get to the door while we are moving?" Red asked.

"With skill," Vanda said. "I will have to pull alongside and you will have to leap for the foot plate."

"But they will see our cart if you move out from behind," she said.

"I will be visible for only a moment. After that, I will fall back and wait for you."

Red looked at that tiny footplate and imagined missing it. She took a deep breath – she could not back out now.

Vanda adjusted his reins and pulled out, heading to the right. The sand was a little softer here, and the cart rocked and juddered. His beasts were alongside the end vehicle now, and that elusive footplate was moving closer.

Red perched on the edge of Vanda's cart, preparing to jump. She looked at Vanda for guidance and he lifted his hand, calling for her to wait. He aimed his carriage as close as he dared and then brought down his hand.

The back door still looked a distance away, but it was now or never. Red leaned forward from under her canopy and launched herself.

The back door had a long, prominent handle, and she caught it with one hand. One of her feet landed on the step, but the other slid off, and for a moment, she hung helplessly, her free arm flailing as she tried to balance. She bounced about and struggled to right herself. Then, with a mighty effort, she brought her other hand about and gripped a small rail next to the door.

Red looked back at Vanda and waved. She was keen to enter the carriage. Her heart filled her chest as she turned the handle. The door opened easily, and she slipped inside.

The interior was very dark and the air stale and humid. Red closed the door behind her to cut out noise.

"White, are you in here?" she whispered.

She shuffled her feet along and soon met with an object. Her hands roamed and found several other obstructions. This was impossible, she told herself.

Red turned and went back to the exit. Vanda had pulled his carriage back in line and now sat patiently behind the sleeping car. The two enormous beasts sniffed the air as they watched her.

"It's too dark," she mouthed, placing her hands over her eyes to show her predicament.

Vanda reached under his seat. Then he threw something at her. Red reached out and caught the item.

What she held was a nightstick. She knew it had three powerful magnifying orbs.

The musky smell of the carriage filled her nostrils once more, and she closed the door behind her.

The interior came to life. Dusty boxes and crates filled the carriage. Something in one of them clucked and shifted. Red moved forward, carefully examining all that she encountered.

The carriage seemed to go on forever. She lifted canvas covers while whispering the name she had in her head. The cart ended, and she had found nothing, but instinct told her she was near.

Red made her way back to let Vanda know she needed more time and that this carriage was a negative. She showed she was moving on. Vanda did not look entirely comfortable, but reluctantly nodded his head and waved her off.

Once again, she navigated the tight interior. At the back stood a narrow door. She opened it and saw a second door across the way. All she had to do was walk across the plank-sized connecting platform. She breathed in and boldly passed from one carriage to the next.

She leaned against this other door and listened. No sound came from inside, so she turned the handle. She did not need a nightstick in this carriage, because a ceiling lamp lit the interior. There, lying on a cot, was her missing crewmember.

Red closed the door behind her and moved forward. The girl lay bound by thick ropes and metal clasps. The travellers had fitted her with some kind of helmet device – switches pulsed and tiny lights flashed.

Moving closer, Red looked through the visor at the face within. The woman had features not unlike her own, pale, slender, with a gentle mouth. White appeared to be sleeping, or something resembling sleep. Red placed her hand on the helmet to absorb the information.

Red shook her head and felt a surge of anger. This device was a suppressor. It kept the person in a coma-induced-state. In addition, the device was ability disabling. The caravan herders were not taking a chance with their precious cargo.

Red moved her hand from the visor to one shackle. This was going to be a problem without the right tools. The shackles had locked cuffs. The cot, however, was weaker. It was old, and she sensed its fragmentations. She looked around for a weapon and then remembered her cannon. Did she dare to use it?

The door to the carriage beyond suddenly flew open. A red-faced man with a wide moustache lunged forward. Red gasped as the man grabbed her wrist.

She pried her arm away, and in doing so, tumbled backwards and landed on the floor. A second man appeared behind her. He clambered forward with eager hands. With an effort, Red reached into her pocket and pulled out her cannon. The sight of it made both men freeze. Their smug faces became a mask of uncertainty.

Red carefully got to her feet. She turned her gun this way and that as she tried to cover both directions.

Both of the men stood poised, like desert vultures, readying themselves for the fight – their eyes were wild, searching for the right moment, their lips displaying clenched teeth.

The carriage suddenly lurched as the caravan came to a halt.

Red fell and nearly dropped her cannon. One man lurched forward. Red brought about her weapon and fired. A blue blast of light shot out, burning a small hole right through the man's chest. He toppled forward, dead. Before she could bring her cannon about, a pair of hands grabbed her from behind.

Her attacker was strong. Two arms wrapped around her chest and squeezed. Red felt all the air leave her lungs. She tried to breathe in, but her ribs could not expand. The man's body pressed against her and his breath was on her neck, sweet with alcohol, his body odour strong and pungent. Her head felt light and her body demanded oxygen. A dizzying sensation washed over her – her hands lost strength and let go of her weapon.

Without warning, the man's arms suddenly relaxed, and Red found she could draw breath. She turned as her assailant fell to the floor. Then she saw Vanda standing there, his arm still raised, his hand holding the bloodied butt of his gun.

Red, still drawing in deep breaths, smiled her gratitude. Suddenly, a searing pain shot up her leg, and she fell to one knee. Vanda cried out as a long piece of metal came sliding through the lower portion of his arm. Then Vanda was clubbed from behind.

Red picked up the cannon and turned to face whoever had shot at her. A man swiftly kicked the gun from her hand and it tumbled across the floor. She gripped her leg and realised a sonic blast had hit her. Luckily, it had been set for stun, rendering her leg only temporarily frozen. Quick as the wind, two men were upon her, dragging her towards the exit. Red looked back and saw a third man heaving Vanda's limp body towards the opposite exit.

The men dragged her past the bunk with her sleeping friend. Some rescuer she had turned out to be, she told herself as they pulled her out of the carriage. Then, as the coolness of the night drifted across her face, other concerns entered her head.

Chapter Twenty-Three

T he two men possessed incredible strength. They dragged her off to a flat patch of sand. One of them, a man with a wide gut, was trying to hold down her leg that was still active, while the other traveller sat across her torso, pressing her upper limbs into the soft sand using his large paw-like hands.

She writhed, but it was no good. All she could do now was move her head, so she tried to remain calm. Thrashing about would only sap her energy. Something, some intuition, told her that there would be another moment, if she stayed still.

The man above her looked down triumphantly. He smiled, displaying lab-grown teeth. Then he leaned further and kissed her forehead. Her situation was about to reach a new level of chaos.

The man above her looked back at his friend and laughed. Red could just about see past him, to this other man. He chuckled as he loosened his belt.

Think, she said to herself. Think your way out of this. She had the idea of shouting that she had an off-planet disease, but they did not seem the type of men to care. Then, her roaming hands dug into the sand and felt something. She touched the objects' smooth curves and realised she had found the nightstick. It must have been in her cloak pocket all this time. She fumbled about and found the switches.

The man above her was still looking back at his friend. He snorted back a laugh, seeing how his travelling companion had caught his belt in a loop.

Red breathed slowly and waited for the right moment.

A noise like a gust of wind suddenly filled the night and then it was gone, as if it was never there. The man above her tensed, His weight shifted, and he fell sideways, blood flowing quickly from his neck. Red looked up just in time to see Vanda come running forward. He came up behind the second man and aimed his smoking gun at his head.

The man sitting astride Red's legs slowly reached inside his tunic. Red saw this and brought up the nightstick. Switching it to full, she aimed it at the man's face. He let out an almighty yelp and fell away, clutching at his blinded eyes.

Now that she was free, she quickly hobbled to her feet and embraced Vanda.

"That's twice you have saved me," she said. Then she looked at his arm and saw the blood.

"You're wounded," she said. Vanda passed her his gun and told her to watch the man. He ripped off a piece of his shirt and wrapped it around his wound.

"Let's take care of him and release your friend," Vanda said.

Hearing this, the man on the ground leapt forward, knocking the gun from Red's hand as he ran away. Vanda quickly retrieved the weapon and aimed it at the fleeing man.

"No, let him go," Red said as she watched the figure clamber across the sand. "He can do us no harm now. Let the desert have him."

Vanda watched the man for a moment longer as he disappeared into the night. He nodded his head in agreement. Then they ambled back along the carriages.

Red entered the cart first and reclaimed her cannon.

"They have a strange array of devices," Vanda said, pointing at the helmet. "This was not a random kidnaping. It looks like they have experience."

Red felt around the head cover and found a catch. Taking a deep breath, she unfastened it and gently lifted it from the girl.

"She is pretty, your sister," Vanda said.

"My sister?" Red replied.

Vanda pointed at the girl. "Can you not see the likeness? I would even be as bold as to say, your twin sister. The resemblance is undeniable."

Red stroked the girl's face and closed her eyes. Her senses could not find out if this was true, but what she could sense was that Vanda was wrong about the age. The girl was younger.

The girl's eyes flickered, but she did not wake.

"Those shackles will be a problem," Vanda said, going down to the attachments and inspecting the silver plates. "They need a special key."

"We have to break them. If we can't, we must attach the carriage to your caravan and tow her."

"Blue, is that you?" a voice said.

White came awake. She blinked several times and then turned her head.

There was that name again, Red thought. She looked at the girl and believed that maybe she *was* her sister.

The girl panicked when she tried to move her arms.

"Do not fear us," Red began. "We are here to help. You are in a caravan and your captors are no more."

The girl inspected Red's face. "Who are you? Why do we look the same?"

"I think this is your sister," Vanda said.

The girl relaxed but did not put her head back down on the pillow. She looked at Vanda and then back at Red. "I have no memory of you," she admitted.

"I have no memory of you, either, save for a handful of fleeting images. Your name is White, is it not?"

The girl nodded her head.

"You called out the name Blue. I too have had that name on my mind – do you know who he is?"

"He is my brother," the girls said. "And if we are sisters, then he must be your brother, too."

Red searched her mind for even the slightest memory, but failed.

"I remember you," the girl suddenly gasped. "You said that everything will be alright."

"When was this?"

"Not here," White replied, looking about.

"We should leave this place before another wagon caravan happens along," Vanda said.

"I'll need a lever to break those bonds," Red said, looking about for an object.

"There's no need," White replied as she pulled at her shackles.

"You will only hurt yourself," Vanda said. "Those shackles are too strong..." but it was too late. A splitting sound filled the compartment as the cot plates ripped from their housing. First, the girl's right hand came free and then the other.

"That isn't possible," Vanda said, looking at the destruction. "No human could do that."

"She's no droid," Red said, surprising herself with her reply.

"If you say so," Vanda said, holding up his hands.

"Trust me, I know," Red said, and felt a little guilty for raising her voice.

White, undistracted, kicked away the last of her shackles and sat up.

Red smiled at her. "You know; you could have saved us a lot of energy by doing that earlier."

White frowned. "Not with that helmet stemming my powers," she said. "My reserves of energy are still low, but that helmet reduced them to nothing."

"Powers – what did I tell you?" Vanda said. "She's different. An anomaly."

White looked at him and smiled. "That is a good way of describing me."

"I think you're going to have to explain things to me, because I really don't understand," Red said.

White looked about. "Are we alone?"

"We are alone," Vanda said.

"Apart from the one that ran away," Red said.

"One of them got away," White said, looking from face to face. "But we can't let him."

The girl got up from the bed, her eyes wide. "We have to catch him."

"Who knows which way he is travelling? The land is not flat – the dusk will mask his passage," Vanda said.

"We cannot allow him to get away," White said again, this time with more emphasis.

Red stood beside her sister and mentally noted how similar in height they were.

"I blinded him," Red admitted, taking no pleasure in imparting this information. "He won't get far. The desert will probably be his downfall."

"Sight or no sight, there's still a slight chance he could send a message saying I escaped. Syrin could intercept that message. They are surely searching for me."

Red shook her head. "Syrin, what is Syrin?"

White looked at her with a puzzled expression. "Syrin is our hell."

Red looked into her eyes and saw fear. Some inner sense told her the word Syrin meant danger, but she did not know why.

Chapter Twenty-Four

T ime was of the essence, and the mystery surrounding Syrin had to wait. White still seemed preoccupied with this missing man, even after Vanda and Red tried to quash her concerns.

Vanda told her that the desert had no frequencies. Communications did not work without specialised equipment, and this man ran away with no such device. To send a signal, he would have to reach a trading post.

"And is there a trading post near?" White asked.

Vanda looked at both of them and faltered. "Yes, there is Stowl. It is near to here."

"Then that's where I must go," White announced, rubbing her wrists.

"But the man's eyes were blinded," Red said. "I don't see how he's a threat."

White shook her head. "Eyes have a way of adjusting, and I can't take that risk. I'm going regardless."

"We can take you there," Red said, looking at Vanda. She had only just found her sister, and she did not want to lose her again.

Vanda shook his head. "I'm so sorry, my friend. This is where we must part. The trading post is a small community with no clinic. I would not trust them with my injury. I need to head for Solar One."

Red remembered his wound and felt guilty. She nodded her head.

"Then we will part. I owe you my life and I will never forget that," she said, placing a hand on his shoulder.

"So you're coming with me?" White said – her expression was one of delight.

Red nodded. "We were both on that shuttle. We must stick together. And maybe, as we journey, you can fill in the blanks that my mind has somehow lost."

"Take two of the lead animals," Vanda said. "They will follow the scent of our runaway."

"I look forward to seeing him again," White said, her features hardening.

• • • • • • • • • •

A short moment later, they stood at the front of the caravan, holding the reins of two beasts. The animals were in an odd alignment, and Vanda was suspicious. He thought the fleeing man had doubled back and took one of the beasts.

"Here, take my night stick. It will be useful, but never use it on the crest of a dune – you might as will light a flare," Vanda said.

Red felt very emotional as she said her farewell. She hoped that one day their paths would meet again. White nodded her head as they mounted their rides. Then they were off, galloping across into the crimson dusk.

The beasts, despite their size, were swift without the heavy wagons to pull. Their heads were down as they ran, their small snouts sniffing the tracks.

"The place you mentioned. We were both there, together?" Red asked.

"You mean Syrin?" White said. "Yes, we were. My memory isn't complete, but I remember some things I overheard." She shook her head. "I can only remember a couple of things about Blue."

"Were we prisoners?"

White thought about it. "I get the impression that it was our home, but one we wanted to leave. And we had all kinds of training. They wanted us ready for something, but that's where my recall gets fuzzy."

At the mention of home, Red had a memory flash. She sat up straight in her saddle and gasped. In her mind's eye, she was lying inside a container, with no way out. She tried to move her arms, to no avail.

"What's wrong?" White asked.

"A container. They sealed me inside."

"I was in a life pod. Is that what you are talking about?"

Red shook her head. "No. The container was slowly filling with a fluid. It was yellow..." then her eyes went wide. "And I had pads and connection wires running everywhere."

White shake her head. "I think that was part of our conditioning. Our training called for it. Someone said that to me, but I can't remember who."

"What kind of training calls for such measures?" Red said, aghast.

White reached over and placed her hand on Red's shoulder, her face furrowed with thought. "There's something else," she said, gazing at her sister's face.

Red gasped and held up her hand, calling for silence. "Sister, we were not born in the usual sense. I mean, not like other people. I think we were... grown."

White shook her head and didn't speak for a while, her mind searching her own flashes of past. "My memory does not recall that, but that would account for all the lab stuff I keep seeing. What I'm sensing is that something changed. They grew angry with us. I can recall angry moments and lots of shouting. I'm sure they now want us dead."

Exhaling, Red looked out at the vast land. "I don't understand any of this, and I'm at a loss for what we did wrong."

White thought about it, searching her own memory for an answer. "Why are our memories so incomplete? Is there something wrong with our heads?"

Red explained about the ruptured tanks and the mix of fuel and gasses.

"But that would only last a very short time," White said.

Red did not answer. It was something that she had not allowed herself to contemplate. The longer that it took for her memory to return, the more that it seemed unlikely the effects were just down to the chemical mix. Some other factor was present, and she did not know what.

"What happens when we've dealt with the traveller?" Red asked, hoping that White had some kind of plan.

"We must find Blue, of course," she said, as if the answer were obvious. "He will know what to do."

"Was Blue in the crash?" Red asked. "I seem to remember someone..."

"He must have been," White said.

"If he's our brother, then why did he leave us?"

White turned her head away as she contemplated the question. A moment of silence followed. "Blue obviously had his reasons. Our brother loves us; he wouldn't just walk away," she said.

Red looked over at her and hoped she was right.

The large dunes vanished, and the sand levelled out. A minor road appeared, just a worn, compressed path, and there in the distance, they saw a small light.

"Is that Stowl?" White asked.

Red considered the question. "No, I don't think so. I would expect more than one light."

"Then maybe it's our runaway?"

Red studied the light. It looked stationary.

The beasts seemed as spritely as ever as they headed along the trail. The tiny glow increased, and they saw that a slender pole housed the light. Beneath this illumination, they saw fresh tracks that had not yet blown away on the wind.

"Vanda was right. Our man was busy while we were rescuing you," Red said, pointing at the floor.

"He's riding a beast?" White said.

Red agreed. "He didn't need to see after all. The beast would know the way – and no wonder we haven't caught him up yet."

They reached the illuminated marker. A display screen, sand-whipped and scratched, stated how far it was to Stowl. They were close. They swapped looks and moved off with a renewed vigour.

Like stars in the sky, several tiny pinpoints of light soon appeared on the horizon. The Sky had the first tinges of yellow and soon the second sun would tip the horizon, shedding its radiant glow.

More lights came into view and they could see several windows. Various outlines of buildings materialised like ghosts. Wind battered silver cargo containers nestled together. People had turned these hulking containers into dwellings. Their sides lay half-buried by thick sand-drifts. Two towers appeared further on. One was some kind of bulbous water container, the other a tall mast.

Two long rows of buildings shadowed the street. The street was devoid of life, as if the entire area lay abandoned. An eatery looked inviting. A couple of single seat sand-cruisers stood outside, but they saw no sign of a tethered beast belonging to their runaway.

A stronger breeze struck up, disturbing sand, which swirled around in circles. They could hear music now and the warm, yellow light seemed far too bright on the eyes.

"Look, there," White said, pointing. Red followed her hand and looked further down. There, next to a liquid trough, stood a single beast.

Red inspected and shook her head negatively. White looked a little dejected.

"Maybe someone inside can tell us if he's been this way," White said.

"We can try," Red replied, glancing at the glow of the hazy windows.

They both dismounted, and walked their rides past the sand-cruisers to another large stone trough. The two beasts dipped their heads and drank. Knowing their beasts were secure, they made their way to the entrance.

The strange music sounded louder once inside. They eyed the room with its sprinkling of people before approaching the long bar. Vast pipes crisscrossed the ceiling. The air, thick with vape-juice smoke, hung like a mist about the soft lighting.

Red, who had experienced two watering holes already, noted White's look of fascination.

Two men sitting on tall bar stools turned and looked at them. One had a big, bushy beard, as fuzzy looking as his long overcoat. His skin looked harsh and wind-dried. The other wore a blue vinyl coat. His arms rested on the bar and his hands gripped his tall drinking tube. Both had googles pushed up onto of their foreheads. They were surely the owners of the two sand-cruisers.

White nudged her and gestured across the way.

The bar was L-shaped and two people, a man and a woman, sat on the other side.

It was impossible to miss the man; he looked the same size as one of their beasts, outside. His baldhead had strange markings that dotted down to his ears. Various trinkets and chains dangled from his beefy arms. The man did not look at them, but his woman, a short, stocky figure dressed in black with a chest that promised to burst free of her tunic, eyed them with suspicion.

White, who had been staring, realised that the short woman was looking back at her. She quickly averted her gaze elsewhere.

Behind the bar, with her back to them, stood a tall, slender woman. She was busy changing one of the dispensing taps. Without looking, she threw the empty cartridge into a bin beside her. The cartridge hit its target and rattled noisily around the container.

"Hello?" asked White, her voice sounding far too young and out of place for such an establishment.

The barperson turned and Red heard her sister stifle a gasp. The woman was not Majarri born. She had a long fluted nose that ended with a rounded chin. Two nostrils twitched, and she looked for all purposes like a cross between a woman and a horse.

"Can I help you?" she asked. Her voice was soft and clear. Her wide, expectant eyes looked at both of their faces.

"Are you... what they call, off-planet?" White asked.

The woman raised one eyebrow. "What rock did you crawl out from?"

White looked at Red, then back to the woman. "We didn't see any rocks, just sand."

The huge bald man sitting around the corner of the bar broke into laughter. The woman at his side did not share in his merriment.

"Look, honey. I can see that you are both kids, so I will not take offence. No, I am not native to Majarri. My name is Jinnica. Welcome to my bar. Now, what can I get you?"

Red leaned forward, placing her hands on the sticky counter. "We are looking for a man," she said.

"Aren't we all," Jinnica said.

"He arrived here a short moment ago."

"Hey, the man you're after had a quick drink and went round the back," said one of the cruiser drivers said. "If you're quick, you'll catch him."

White nudged her sister and motioned to leave. Red was about to move away from the bar when the stallion-faced woman seized hold of her wrist.

"Don't listen to him," she whispered. "They are not good men. There has not been a man on his own in here tonight. They only want to lure you around the back."

Jinnica leaned back and looked down the bar to the two cruiser drivers. "You should think before you talk, my friend. You might find yourself back on the road before you have finished your drinks."

At that moment, another man came striding down from the back of the room. It was easy to tell which group he belonged. He had the same baldhead with dotted markings. He joined the giant and his woman and sat down. Then he noticed Red and her sister, and his eyes narrowed.

"You won't throw us out," the cruiser driver said to the woman behind the bar. "You like our credits. And this dump needs all the credits it can get."

"That wasn't very nice, trying to trick us," Red heard White say. She had been studying the two cruiser drivers, but now she noticed how her sister was standing away from the bar, addressing the driver.

"Simmer down short stuff – you're not even my type," the driver said, picking up his drinking tube.

"The two of you come in here, thinking you're fancy," the other driver said, looking past his friend. "You're probably one of these rich kids on a travelling kick. People like you make me sick."

"More of that talk and you are out," Jinnica said before turning to Red and her sister. "Unless you want to eat or drink, I suggest you leave as well. You're disturbing my clientele."

"They already look disturbed," White said, still focusing on the drivers.

"Someone needs a lesson from daddy," the cruiser driver said, rising from his stool.

"We are leaving," Red announced, holding her hands up. She did not want a scene. They knew now that the traveller had not been here, so it was time to leave.

The man with the long vinyl coat started advancing. Now his friend was also rising from his seat, his hands flexing as he stood.

"Hey, guys, I don't want no trouble," the woman said from behind the bar.

The cruiser driver looked at her as he advanced. "No trouble here. Just putting some rich kids in their place."

The bar woman moved quickly along the bar and grabbed hold of the man's arm. "Hey, how about a round on me, and your friend over there, if he takes his seat again?"

The man looked sideways, "What do you say to that, Astell?" he said, with a smirk.

His friend, who had gone over to block the doorway, took a quick glance outside through the small porthole and then turned his attention back to his friend. "I'll pass on that one," he said, "Liquid here tastes like piss." Then he pointed. "And I want this kid to learn a lesson."

Red moved herself to stand in front of White. "We meant no harm. All we want to do is leave."

Before either man could reply, White stepped out from behind Red.

"We were having a conversation with Jinnica until you opened your dusty mouth."

Red turned and waved her hand at White, motioning her to be silent.

The man at the door suddenly stepped forward, but his friend held up his hand. "I've got this one, Astell," he said, loosening his jacket.

Jinnica suddenly slapped a slender tube of yellow liquid down on the counter. "Here, stop and have that drink and we'll call it even. What do you say?"

The man looked at the woman with contempt and pushed the tube away. It fell off the bar and landed with a clatter, spilling the contents across the floor.

Red stepped forward and put out her hands, hoping to stop the man. He knocked her aside. Red, too, landed on the floor.

Shaking her head, Red rose, but it was too late. The man had reached her sister. The man at the door shouted crude suggestions. Jinnica went to a panel and hit the security call. Further down the bar, one of the heavy looking men shouted at the driver, telling him to pick on someone his own size. The man by the door suddenly got out a small blaster and aimed it at the giant, silencing him.

The man standing before White slapped her hard across the face with the back of his hand. White stumbled sideways and had to grab the bar to stop herself falling. Then she returned her gaze to the waiting man. A wave of fear gripped Red – but then she saw how her sister was looking at the driver – and White smiled.

The look on White's face was enough to make the driver pause. He looked at that pale face and faltered. The girl's eyes were turning black and her smile looked menacing.

White touched her lip with the tip of her finger and checked for blood and found nothing, but her lip was swelling. Without warning, White's hand cut through the air like a blade. The man instinctively brought his hands up to defend himself, but not quickly enough.

The side of White's hand met with the man's neck. His head snapped back. Everyone heard the connection, even above the music. Then the man was tumbling backwards, clutching his windpipe. Even as he landed on the floor, Red could see that he was choking.

The man standing by the door shuffled forward with his gun held out before him.

White bent over and swung her foot up and over in a quick arc, kicking the gun from the man's hand before he squeezed the trigger. White was still twisting on the spot. Her outstretched hand connected with the man's face, slapping the bridge of his nose. The driver spun and White grabbed hold of him and shoved his head forward – his head hit the counter with a smack. He went down quickly and lay there, his eyes open but lifeless, his forehead already turning a deep purple and his ears leaking a yellowish liquid.

Red noted everything – the suddenness of White's movements, the look upon the watching drinkers, the way the second driver went down and then her sister's black coloured eyes, which were now turning back to their original colour – it was unbelievable.

The bar woman with the long horse face suddenly dived into action.

"I want you out," she said, her gaze not leaving White's face. "You are not right."

At that moment, two men came tumbling in from outside, bringing wind and sand with them. They looked around at the clientele and then down at the two men lying on the floor.

"It's over," the bar woman quickly announced to the site security.

The two men looked at her questioningly. "What happened here?" one of them asked.

"A fight broke out. One of them hit this girl," Jinnica said, pointing at White. She was talking quick now before anyone had the chance to speak. "A couple of men intervened. I do not know who they were. They fought the men you see lying here and left."

One of the security men was leaning over the fallen man.

"He's dead. The other one looks the same," he said, straightening. "You say that a couple of men did this and left?"

"Exactly, Satiff. They came in, saw this drunk lash out at the girl, and started a fight. If it were not for them, then who knows what would have happened. Then they ran."

"Let's see your security footage," the other guard said, pointing up at a tiny camera.

"Monrat is right," Satiff said, rubbing at his jaw and nodding his head.

The bar woman waved a hand, her long face looking a shade paler. "Satiff, that thing hasn't worked in nearly a year. I keep it as a deterrent. Besides, that's why I pay you."

The guard looked at her and shook his head. "Well, isn't this fine, Jinnica," he said. "The main street surveillance for this section is down as well. Seems we had a power surge in the night." He looked down at the two bodies and scratched his temple. "I don't know what we're going to do about his."

Jinnica suddenly reached out and gripped Satiff's arm, peering at him intently. "We don't need to make a big deal out of this, do we?" she said. "We take care of our own here, don't we?"

Satiff looked at her for a moment. "This is a pretty big deal, Jinnica. This ain't no bar-room brawl. We have never had to deal with anything like this. Shit, I don't want to spend the next couple of days listening as Agents interview us.

"Just get rid of them," one of the big men across the way shouted. "Dirty cruisers are always trouble."

"So what did you see?" Monrat asked.

"Me... I didn't see nothing," the giant replied. "Me neither," the other man added, picking up his drink.

The guard stepped over to White. Red observed the man as he inspected her sister's swollen lip. "Is that what happened? They punched you in the face?"

White now looked as she was before, a rather pale-faced young girl with delicate pale eyes. She nodded her head serenely.

"Where are you heading?"

Red cleared her voice. "We're travelling to Solar 1."

The guard turned to face her. He did not look comfortable.

"Just dump the bodies in the desert and have done with it," one of the big men said. "Nobody is going to miss them."

"You seem pretty keen to dispose of them?" Monrat said.

"Those two were all kinds of wrong. One of them has a Rat patch on his arm. The Rats don't run this way anymore, but when they did, you knew about it. Nobody is going to miss that one, you'll see."

The security man looked at the person lying on the floor and then at Red and her sister. He shook his head. His co-worker went over and asked the two big men to hold out their hands. He inspected their knuckles for redness and turned to his companion.

"Wasn't these guys," he said.

The security man sighed as he approached the bar. "I don't know what happened here. I don't think calling this one in will solve the puzzle, either – but this cannot happen again, understand. This never happened." Then the security man looked across at the two men and the short woman. "If we... sort this out. It means you saw nothing as well. If it comes out, you will be an accessory. Comprehend?"

The group across the way nodded and did not voice any concern.

Jinnica slapped two drinks down on the table. Then she turned to Red.

"Go," she said. "Go now and never come to this bar again."

"Thank you," Red said to the woman as she helped her sister to stand.

"Hey, wait," one of the security men said. "What did your friend say to these guys to make them attack her?"

Red looked at the man. "Nothing," she said. "She said nothing."

The man stared at them for a moment longer, his eyes narrowing as he considered her response. Then he picked up his drink and took a sip. "I guess he didn't like your face."

"Where did you say you're heading?" the other man asked.

"We're going to Solar 1," Red replied.

"Look; this place is really for traders, not kids looking for a place to drink. Do yourself a favour and forget about this place. I don't care to see either of you around here again. Got it?"

Red and her sister nodded their heads. "We will be on our way as soon as we rest our rides," Red said.

"You do that," the guard replied, turning back to his drink.

Red left the building with her sister and walked into the growing sunlight. A strong wind had struck up, making the sand scatter loosely across the ground. She knew they both had abilities, but White's abilities were scaring her.

Chapter Twenty-Five

T he night had been long and Manark's troubled mind had given him restless sleep. Morning arrived, and he shuffled around his apartment, going from room to room, trying not to think about what had happened at Syrin the previous day.

The view from his large window on the ninth floor told him the weather looked good. He looked out as Trillian changed with the shifting light. The night workers and the sub-level food emporiums were now either closing or changing shifts. Streetlights that aided the weaker of the two suns turned off as the brightness increased. The new sun drowned out all but the hardiest of shadows.

He sat down again but soon grew restless – he did not feel the slightest bit tired, but his skin felt tight and his chest ached. Manark took a shot of D900, just to smooth himself out. Hell, at least half the city operated on D900.

He looked around the room and decided that the apartment felt oppressive.

He got up and grabbed his jacket. "Lock door after leaving," he said to the voice recognition as he walked down the short hallway. The system repeated the command as Manark opened the door and left the apartment.

The noise of the city greeted him. He hit the black pavement and walked. A gentle breeze caressed his forehead, teasing his thinning fringe. A hover-bus silently drifted along and announced to the pedestrians that it was about to stop. Above him, some twenty feet up – various anti-gravity vehicles waited at the air-signals, their shining expensive panels gleaming, their propulsions ticking and hissing expectantly, and above them, roamed a mass of cargo vessels, and lesser crafts that could not afford to fly so low.

It felt good to be walking – he found the distractions soothing. He came to a crossing and looked both ways. The walk light flashed negative, so he waited with the other pedestrians. He glanced at the hollo-billboards. His favourite one appeared. It showed a woman pouring the latest synthetic brand into a glass. The slogans danced, proclaiming that this new mixture was healthier than ever. He knew the slogan by heart, which gave him more time to study the radiant face of the model. If the woman were genuine, he would like to meet her, just to see what kind of person she was. He looked at the smiling face and imagined having a date with her.

The image suddenly changed, and the speakers crackled into life. "Better than you could imagine, better than you could need... better than the rest," the voice boomed.

Manark's smile dropped as he watched the rolling advert. It was an infomercial about how the latest droids could improve your life. The screen showed a family man with his two children walking along with a female droid. They were holding hands and the man could not have looked happier. Then an image of a woman appeared, standing by her car while a male droid fitted a displacement hose. His smile was warm and friendly, and the woman looked longingly into his eyes.

The law prohibited the advertisement for sex models, but this did not stop the short ad-vids from hinting. The screen-shot changed again, and now a man was sitting up in bed while a synthetic came alongside with a drink. She was wearing a thin nightdress and the message could not have been more blatant as she leaned over and kissed him.

The screen altered and now the Syrin logo appeared and a voice-over said, "Syrin, giving the people perfection."

"You're blocking the way, pal," a voice said, breaking Manark's spell. Looking round, he saw people were now crossing. He entered the swell and moved with the masses.

His breathing felt laboured and his chest restricted. When he reached the other side of the street, a sudden panic gripped him. The advert had rekindled his need to do something – anything.

Manark looked about. He felt lost and in needed of help. He kept on thinking about the three experimental subjects. They were all destined for extermination and it was his name on the document. In saving his own hide, he had signed a death warrant.

Then Manark remembered the Conciliator bar on grid five. He looked at the time counter on the side of a building and knew that it had opened. Sometimes, when he finished a late shift, he would go to that bar and take up residence. The barman, Tocko 6, had always been a comfort. He was an advanced droid, and his programming meant he was a good listener. His counselling programs had helped Manark work through many a dilemma. If anyone would know what to do, it was surely Tocko 6.

After a short walk and a connector-tunnel, Manark arrived at the Conciliator. It looked little from the outside, but the place was a haven away from the city bustle. The lighting bathed the interior in calm greens and cool blues. Artificial foliage and running water complimented the place, giving it an exotic feel. At this time of the morning, it was only half-full – mostly with night workers, keen to forget their shift.

Three droids worked at the bar today. Two were females, sympathetically dressed, not too smutty but enough to complement their figures. The third was Tocko 6. His synthetic casing imitated the best features of many cultures, making him pleasing to all. He had a medium build, not too slim, not too muscular. Again, the effect was charming. He had poise and his polished looks entertained the women while retaining his "average Joe" persona for the male clientele.

"Hello my friend," Tocko 6 said, holding his hand up in recognition.

"Hello to you," Manark said, pressing a foot switch – he waited while a stool rose from the floor.

"Hard work last night?" Tocko 6 asked, producing a tube and wiping it with a cloth.

"I've been up all night, but I haven't been to work," Manark said, taking a seat.

"Oh," said the barman, his face suddenly furrowed with concern. "Are you unwell?" he asked.

"Only in mind," Manark replied with a smile, and before the barman could reply, added, "I'm wrestling with some heavy thoughts."

"Usual tipple?" Tocko 6 asked. Manark nodded. Then, as the barman poured silver-coloured liquid into a drinking tube, added, "Speak up my friend, tell your barman and maybe I can help."

Manark waved a hand in the air as he took his drink. "Oh, you don't need me taking up your time," he said.

The barman gave a shrug of his carefully sculpted shoulders and held out his hands. "Do you see me rushed off my feet? You'd be doing me a favour. My shift will pass more quickly," he said, his delicate accent making his words dance in the air.

Manark gripped his tube with both his hands and contemplated where to begin. He smiled. He needed to be discreet in case anyone walked past. It was a big city, but you could not tell who worked for who.

"You remember I work in bio-insertions," he said, glancing at the barman. The barman nodded accordingly. "Well, I've encountered a moral dilemma."

"Those are the worst dilemmas," Tocko 6 said, picking up another empty tube to rub with his static cloth.

"Well, after five years of programming, the firm that I've worked for has issued three terminations."

Manark felt safe in what he was saying. Syrin, although one of the largest distributers of droids, was not the only company on the market, so he was not naming names.

"Termination?" the barman said.

"Oh, I forgot to mention. I'm talking about three AIs." Manark said.

Despite his programing, Tocko 6 physically reacted. Modern droids possessed thousands of reaction afflictions. He slowed his polishing and his eyes fixed upon Manark.

"So," Tocko 6 said after a moment, "did they pose a threat? Did they break programming?"

Manark thought hard about his answer.

"On paper, yes, but it was I that educated them and I'm telling you that there should not be a problem."

Tocko 6 took another tube and rubbed it down with his cloth. "These corporations don't take terminations lightly. There are genetic rights for droids now. Documents must show the need for extermination. I cannot see an independent party signing something so final."

Manark looked down at his drink. He fumbled with his tube and sighed.

"It was I that signed the assessment." Then he held up his hand. "They made me do it. I would have been in breach of my contract had I not signed. The punishment is two years' stasis."

"That is not a pleasant situation," the droid said, shaking his head. "But tell me. What makes you agonise over their demise? What makes you think the droids had no problems? Machines today can fool people and have many issues."

"No, no." Manark said, shaking his head. "I'm not telling you the full story. You're only aware of the tech that's already on the market." Manark leaned closer and whispered. "These were prototypes... they were different."

Tocko 6 frowned. "How so?"

Manark looked both ways. "What I am about to say, I want you to erase from your memory once I've left." Tocko 6 nodded his head and Manark knew this would happen.

He took a deep breath and kept his voice low. "These were different. They are the missing link between man and AI. Yes, they are a sum of parts, but their parts are not synthetic, but organic. They have organically fused every fibre they possess. They are living beings."

The droid before him stood silent, as he comprehended what Manark was saying.

"They impregnated these units with various drugs and info that no droid could usually absorb. A synthesised body – even an organically grown one, would reject some things that these synthetics have had to endure – but these AIs *have* survived.

After a moment, Tocko 6 spoke again. "But just because they are a first-of-their-kind, it does not mean that they are infallible. In fact, it means that they are more likely to have problems, problems that you may not know about, but that the company could."

Manark shook his head. "I appreciate what you're saying, but I spent five years watching them grow in personality. I tell you that despite what the... the company has done; these AIs are good people."

"People?" the barman said, clearly taken aback. "I've heard no one talk about an AI as a person."

"Well, they are. That is my dilemma. Killing these individuals would be a crime and I feel responsible."

"And it was your word that made this happen?" Tocko 6 asked.

Manark looked at the barman and lowered his voice. "It was." Whatever the droid was thinking, he kept hidden.

"So what are you going to do?" Tocko 6 asked.

Manark shrugged his shoulders. "I really do not know."

"You clearly feel uncomfortable with the knowledge. You seem to want to fix the problem."

"There lies my dilemma," Manark admitted. "I don't work for them anymore. My contract ended."

"Then that is what you must tell yourself," Tocko 6 replied.

A woman further down the bar called for service and the barman winked at Manark and walked away. The wink told Manark that he would return once he had served the woman.

This brief interlude gave Manark time to think. He drank his liquid and contemplated the situation.

The barman finished serving the person and returned.

"So," Tocko 6 said, taking up the conversation. "I have a hypothetical for you."

Manark looked at him and waited.

"Imagine that they force a man into signing a termination and he can't rest until he finds a resolve. He feels so frustrated about the situation that it is eating-him-up. Then why doesn't he use what power he has to foil the big company?"

Manark shook his head. Now he knew that deep down inside the droid's carefully tailored cortex, he did not want these AIs dying.

"What could a man with limited power do? Especially if he isn't working for the firm and he doesn't even know where these AIs are."

"Unless he can live with the fact of their demise, then the answer is simple... he does what he can."

Manark looked at the barman. He observed his face as he had never done before. Yes, he was a sum of many parts. His optical orbits were sensor activated and right now, thirty or more synthetic muscles were operating, but there seemed more to him than just his build-quality. He had reacted humanely. His reaction was far more human than some scientists Manark had worked with.

He nodded his head. "You are right. I know, deep down inside, what I must do. And I must do all that I can."

The barman studied Manark for a moment, and then he smiled and leaned forward. "A person doesn't know what they are capable of until it challenges them."

Manark drained the last of his juice and brushed away the tube. He stood up and placed his credit disk on the counter.

Tocko 6 waved his hand and gave the disk back. "The drink is on me," he said. Then he wiped the bar with one swift flick of his rag and smiled. "If I see you in here again, it will be a triumphant day."

Manark gave the droid a gentle salute, picked up his credit disk and walked away from the bar.

Chapter Twenty-Six

The wind was growing stronger as Red led her sister away from the drinking establishment. When they were a safe distance away from the main doors, Red pulled her sister aside and pushed her against a wall.

"What are you playing at?" she said. "You put us in a dangerous situation – and I thought you wanted to catch our caravan herder. You jeopardised our safety."

White pulled her hands away. "I couldn't help it," she said. "They were no-good gutter-dwellers. They deserved all that they got."

"We can't afford to be so visual. We need to travel like ghosts, do you understand?"

"OK, I'm sorry," White said. "I won't let it happen again."

"The next time it does, I'll leave you to it."

"Like I needed you," White replied, her lip curling.

"Oh, you had it all under control," Red responded. "You have something going on inside you, something I don't understand. And what makes you so dangerous, is that you don't understand it either."

"It's no different to your powers," White said.

"I don't have powers like that," Red admitted. Then she frowned. "And if you have these powers, how come they captured you back in Solar 3?"

White looked uncomfortable as she remembered. "I... I could not access them. I couldn't even remember that I possessed powers," she said.

Red nodded her head, her anger reducing. "I had the same experience."

"But don't you see?" White began, her face brightening. "You have the same powers as I do. You just have to access them. I feel mine growing all the time, and I don't know why."

Red reminded her sister about the gasses at the crash site and how she had been exposed longer. Then she shook her head. "You're wrong about our powers – we have different abilities. Mine is more practical. I have an instant understanding of most things that I touch, whereas you seem to be... a fighting machine."

"I don't like the word machine," White said.

Red remembered how Vanda had said that White could be a droid – and if her sister was not human, it must mean that... she put the notion out of her mind and averted her gaze. "Let's haul out."

The buildings stretched out and most either seemed closed or out of business. They found a trading post, with its fine array of animal skins and parts depot, but they did not hang about to investigate. A little way ahead, they found the communications room, which stood next to a comm tower. They cautiously entered the comm room and hoped that their runaway was waiting.

A man came out from the back room. He walked up to the short counter and smiled as if they were returning friends.

"Hello," he said. "Going to be a stormy day."

"We're looking for someone," White began, but Red quickly silenced her with a squeeze of her shoulder.

"I'm sorry, my sister is impatient," Red began. "We need to communicate with our friend. We gave him a message to send, but we have changed our plans and need to correct the communication."

The slender man's smile vanished. His eyes considered them carefully.

"We can pay for your service," Red added.

"No communications today," the man said.

"So he hasn't been in?" Red asked.

"Nobody been in here for the last two days – but that's not what I meant." He gesticulated towards the window. "We had a power surge – can't say when, but your friend never came here, so I guess he hasn't sent it. A repair unit is on its way."

Red relaxed at hearing this news.

"So there is absolutely no way of sending a message?" White asked.

"There is only one way, but it's difficult," the man said.

Red frowned. "Please explain."

"I have a portable device. It is old, but it still works. The problem is getting a signal on the thing – you'd have to get up high... real high."

"You mean, climb the tower outside?" White said.

The man shook his head and waved away her words. "No, no. Get yourself killed. No, that would not do – too much current running through the thing. Close to here is an old mine on a hill. That would be my choice – gets real high up there, on some of that equipment."

"A mine?" Red echoed. "Out here?"

The man nodded. "Some company, many years ago, scanned the area and found amazing results – the area was rich in crystals, or at least, that's what their research said." The man waved his hand in the air. "Load of old toxic. They found crystal fragments, no bigger than grains of sand. The rock bed in this region is full of it. Enough to give false readings. They abandoned the mine when they discovered the truth. The buildings here were originally for the workers. You know, club house, sleeping quarters."

"So our friend may have gone there?" Red asked.

"It would be no good without my equipment," the man said. "Here, I'll go get it to show you."

The man disappeared into the back. Red and her sister exchanged looks but said nothing.

The man came back a short moment later, but he was not carrying the communication device. He was carrying an energy blaster.

"Don't move a muscle," he said. "I smelt trouble when you walked in and I wasn't wrong."

Red put her hands up. "What do you mean?"

"What has happened?" White asked.

"You know exactly what has happened," the old man said, keeping his sights turned on them. "You come in here asking about communications at the moment that my gear goes for a walk. Just a coincidence, I suppose?"

"It's our friend. He must have taken it," White said.

"So, a man I didn't see took it. How convenient," the man said, moving the twin barrel from face to face. He came around the counter, moving with caution.

Red was getting angry at the man's logic. "Well, you're implying that we took it and you didn't see us take it, either."

The man gritted his teeth. "I want it returned."

Red glanced at her sister and noticed how her irises were dilating until her eyes looked like solid pools of black.

The old man behind the counter noticed the change in White as well, and his mouth fell open. His hands were shaking.

White's movements were now so quick that neither the man nor her sister had time to react. One minute, the man was holding the gun, and then he had lost it. She was so quick that the man's finger broke as it snagged on the trigger. The man cried out in pain and clutched his hand.

White looked at her sister and shrugged.

The man was hopping around in pain as Red took the gun from her sister's hands.

"Tell us about the mine," Red said.

"There's nothing to tell," he replied between pants.

"Is there only one shaft, or more?" White asked.

"Two, I think. I have not been up there in many years. No need to."

"What part of the mine is best for communication?"

The man stopped his prancing. He stood there, clutching his finger, his face grimacing. He seemed reluctant to reply until Red lifted the gun further and aimed. "There's an old hydraulic crane. He might climb that," the man said.

"Sister, what's that in your hand?" Red asked, making the old man turn to look at White. The trick worked, and with the old man surprised, Red twirled the gun about and hit the man on the forehead with the butt of the weapon. He fell to the floor, unconscious.

"Now who's being violent?" White said to her sister.

"That was a tactical move – there is a difference," Red replied, motioning for them to get moving.

When they left the Comm Office, the swirling sand storm had increased. Red put up her hood and White pulled her top over her mouth. Then Red pointed back the way they came, and White followed her gaze.

Through a sandy-haze came several figures. It was the two guards. Evidently, the old man had done more than just grab his gun when he was in the back – he had raised an alarm. The guards were on their way with a couple of people in tow. They did not look like they were out for a casual stroll, either.

"This way," Red shouted above the wind.

They ran into the storm and away from the main street. Eventually, they reached the last of the buildings. Up ahead were the remains of an old wire fence, and beyond that, up a steep incline, lay the dark outline of the resting mine.

Chapter Twenty-Seven

The terrain was tough and the rise steep, but they eventually reached the first of the mine buildings. Red looked back to see if the guards were still coming their way, but the storm was gaining in strength, and it reduced the outpost to a faint outline.

A couple of huts appeared. An insignia, bleached with time, displayed a company logo. The door to the hut was long gone. Inside was a long table.

With nothing to gain from the hut, they continued, searching the many buildings as they went.

An abandoned machine lay across their path, its wheels and pulleys battered by sand and wind. Machine parts littered the floor. Beyond that stood a cage-like structure. A top-hatch swung precariously in the wind. Old rusting cables hung like creeping vines.

Red nudged her sister and motioned with her head. White looked and saw the crane. She studied it for a moment, expecting to see movement. Then Red pointed over towards a large control cabin that hung from the end of the structure. If their man were trying to send a signal, it would be from there.

"Do you think we are in time?" White asked.

"Maybe," Red replied. "Who knows, way out here? He may not have been successful, not with portable equipment."

White stared back at her with a renewed optimism. Red looked at the height of the crane, and knew they had to climb up and look in the control box. She was not looking forward to it.

· · · ● · ● · ● · ·

Manark had returned home. He still had his old program card, but had Syrin really turned off his access code? he wondered.

This was just one of his dilemmas. The other was more complicated. He knew he had to help the three AIs and that meant finding them. If anyone knew their whereabouts, it was Syrin. He needed that info. His plan was simple – let the AIs know exactly what they were and let them release their true potential. After that, it seemed simple. With his help, they could infiltrate Syrin and take control, or better still, destroy the research centre along the mother-frame that held all the data. Then they could disappear. Well, it was not exactly simple, but once they knew what they were, the rest would fall into place.

Manark felt confident that the front desk would recognise him, knowing that his contract had ended. But the security at the service personnel entrance had never seen him before.

He left his building. He travelled to a specific store that specialised in work clothing. All the corporations bought from this shop. Finding a match for a Syrin service worker would not be a problem. The only thing missing was the logo or the hologram badge. He would face that hurdle when it presented itself.

The store had a wide variety of work garments. He knew that the maintenance people wore long green jackets. The jackets he found looked the right shade, but for remembering what kind of footwear they wore, his mind drew a blank. Manark took a chance and bought what he could.

He paid and left the building before he had time to contemplate what he was doing.

The quick trip across town on the shuttle made his stomach turn uneasily. He clutched his bag of clothing and tried to steady his breathing. The only thing that was getting him through this ordeal was the thought of preventing three terminations – that and the look on Sarak's face when her three experiments stood in front of her.

He got off the shuttle bus and walked towards the building. He journeyed down the maintenance ramp towards the services entrance.

The door was unattended when he arrived. The general shift pattern would have already begun for most. Some lower-level employees would filter through from time to time, but right at that moment, all seemed still.

He walked up to the scanner and held up his old ID card. The scanner bleeped, but the door did not open.

"I'm sorry, but there seems to be an imperfection with your card today," a synthetic female voice said. "Please input your security number or try again with a different card."

Manark swallowed. A panel had flipped open, revealing a key pad. He copied his code from the back of the card.

"I'm sorry, but the code you have tried does not match," the voice said. "Would you like me to call for help? Press 1 for yes, 2 for no."

Manark pressed two. Then he tried to recall his older code. Surely, after his breach the other day, that code would be invalid as well.

Lifting his shaking hand, he typed. Closing his eyes, he tried to remember the numbers and letters. He had created a rhyme to remember the digits, but his recall was vague. Twice he hit the delete key and retyped.

"You have twenty seconds remaining to finish your transaction," the voice said. "After that, I will notify a security team," the monotone voice declared.

He cursed as he quickly finished inputting and pressed on the return.

"Code accepted for... Manark," the voice announced as the door slipped open.

Manark exhaled and entered the building, not daring to believe that the code had not alerted security. This was a huge oversight on the company, but then again, there were so many agencies providing service personnel, not to mention specialised short-term project workers. The corridor ahead was empty. He wiped beads of sweat from his forehead as he walked. His footwear sent gentle echoes around the clean walls.

He did not know about this sector's protocol. What he knew was that maintenance employees did not leave the building wearing their uniforms – there had to be changing rooms. As if to answer his question, he noticed a sign for the male dressing sector.

He walked into the room and found he was not alone. A man looking just a couple of years his junior looked up before resuming his dressing.

Manark smiled as he placed his bag on a seat. He tried to still his shaking hands. Then he spied a chart on the wall. It showed the various workers and their work areas. It also listed the level of decontamination needed for that employee. General maintenance personnel only needed to wash hands and slip on foot covers. Manark relaxed. He had seen a box of such items on the way in.

Manark slipped on his green coat and headed to a locker. He stashed his own jacket and took a pair of white over-boots.

He left the changing room and walked down the corridor, his foot covers making swishing noises against the smooth floor. At the other end of the hall was a door with a large tinted panel. Manark could see a security man, who was busy tapping at his info pad. This was it, Manark thought as he opened the door.

The deskman looked up as Manark entered the lobby. Manark grabbed his shoulder and massaged the area. He rolled his neck from his to side as if he had muscular discomfort, his hand and his forearm hiding the absence of a company logo.

"Another day in paradise," he said to the man.

"Tell me about it," the security person muttered as he looked back at his pad.

Manark felt far too hot. A sign on the wall made him stop in his tracks. The sign read left for maintenance, cleaners and food preparers, and an arrow pointing to the right simply stated all other operatives. Turning right would eventually lead him to areas that he knew, including the labs, but his clothing did not permit him to take this direction.

His luck had just run out. If he turned right, the guard would notice. If he turned left, he would enter a maintenance depot. Manark knew nothing of the daily maintenance routine and felt assured his deception would fall apart.

He stood for a moment, contemplating whether to make a dash for it, or turn around and say he had forgotten something important from his vehicle. Then he heard voices and turned.

"You're late," the desk operative said, turning to look at a man who had come through the opposite door. "You're cutting into my break."

It was a security changeover. The replacement turned to look at the wall clock, as did the desk man, who followed his gaze, shaking his head. Manark did not wait to see the rest of their conversation. He quickly took a right turn and dashed down the corridor.

Manark reached a second junction and inched forward. The corridor was empty. A changing room came into view and he entered. Peering around the door, he heard a shower running in the next room. A cubicle was vacant, and he quickly discarded his work coat. Then, after checking that the coast was still clear, he went over to an empty locker and hid the item of clothing.

Old habits were hard to shake as he started a cleansing process. Then he chose one of the long white disposable jackets and exited.

He knew several labs well, and he tried to work out which one would best suit his needs. Then he had an idea – it was a crazy thought.

He turned towards Sector 7 with a scary hypothesis raging through his mind. When he last worked here, they were closing down a section. After a project ended, they moved the scientists and the lab technicians on to other areas. Syrin's vast complex made it possible for section closures. Then, when a new project started, a lab rebuild would happen. The project had only just disbanded, so the lab that had housed the Arin project might still be intact.

Sector 7 had two sizable labs. Manark walked down the hallway with a growing unease. He rubbed his hands together. The area ahead was free from traffic.

It had been a long time since he had been in these labs. If he had known what he knew now, he would have helped the AIs escape. Syrin was breaking every kind of code in wanting the three test subjects destroyed. His worry was that nobody knew of the AIs' existence. He was their only hope. They were running around blind, not understanding the danger they faced, and not understanding what they truly were. Mind programing could do that, leave gaping holes that blocked the bigger picture – it made it easier for additional inputs.

There it was. A little way ahead was the sign for Sector 7, Lab B. He approached with caution. His hand nervously fumbled in his pocket for the card. Cautiously, he looked down the corridor – it remained empty – then he looked left, straight into the eyes of an oncoming operative.

Manark turned his attention back to the scan panel.

"Manark, is that you?" the woman said.

He recognised the voice. She was a biomaterial scientist, specialising in body coverings – at least that was what she had been doing five years ago.

"Well hello there… Dr …?"

"Dr Crinley," she replied, a warm smile spreading across her face. "Don't worry, it has been quite a while," she added, trying to ease his embarrassment at not recalling her name.

Manark smiled. He was still holding his swipe card out before him. He did not want to start up a big conversation, and so he waited for her to speak.

"So, how have you been?" she asked, filling the silence between them.

"Oh, you know, same old, same old." He grinned and fell silent again.

Dr Crinley got the message that he was not in a talkative mood. It looked like she was about to say her goodbyes when she glanced up at the nameplate on the wall.

"Oh, I thought they had abandoned this project?"

Manark looked at the sign and back at her face. "Oh, yes... yes, they have. Just recently, actually. I am here as part of the shutdown. You know, they want me to clear out any sensitive information."

Crinley looked at him for a moment, and Manark felt himself blush. It was a lame excuse, spoken in haste and without thought. Clearance was the job for a tech team – he knew it and he was sure that Crinley knew this as well.

She tutted and shook her head. "They will keep giving us more and more to do. One day they will ask us to clean the floors before we leave."

Manark laughed a little too heartily, and his cheeks blushed further. Then he looked down at his access card. "Well, if you don't mind," he said. "I have a lot to do."

"Oh, no, I totally understand," the woman said, waving a hand before her. "I've just finished my break.

Must get back myself." She absently brushed a hand through her hair and averted her eyes, as if distracted.

Manark held his card up to the panel. He hoped his card was still lab-active. Dr Crinley nodded and walked away.

The access light turned green and Manark opened the door. Looking down the corridor, he noticed the scientist turning her head in his direction. He waved, and she waved back. Manark couldn't help but notice the quizzical look on her face. Then he went inside and quickly closed the door behind him. Exhaling, he pressed his back to the door. This was possibly the craziest day of his life. A dark, vacant lab lay before him.

Chapter Twenty-Eight

S plintered timbers and rusting drums lay scattered around the foot of the crane. They picked their way across dented cylinders, old tarpaulins and ropes, and coils of thick hose. White was in the lead, climbing nimbly over the debris. She was far more agile, Red noted as she struggled to maintain her footing, and slipped several times.

White was too far ahead.

"Wait for me," Red said, watching the figure of her sister become a grey shape amid the swirling sands. She quickly realised White could not hear her above the hiss of the wind. The storm was growing in strength. Maybe the man they were chasing could not send a signal after all – but she reminded herself how long he had been up there. His message could have been sent long before the storm started – Syrin, keen to find any sign of them, might intercept his message and deploy a team. All these thoughts and more turned uneasy in her mind.

White had already reached the ladder, and climbed several feet up, as Red reached the base. She took hold of the ladder and paused. A gaping pit yawned right beside the crane. Red stared at it for a moment before starting after her sister.

The climb was slow. Old hydraulic lubricant had been leaking from above for some time, coating parts of the ladder in a greasy slime. The wind was getting stronger, disturbing small pieces of rubbish and sending them up into the air. This did not seem to impede her sister, who had nearly reached the top. White was like a monkey, quickly pulling herself up onto the long arm of the crane.

Red stopped. Her impatient sister was too far in front now. She just hoped that if the man was in the control box, he had not gained a weapon.

Looking down, Red could just make out the open maw of the pit. One wrong step and she would go sailing down into the hole, and that would be the end. This was not how she had envisaged their plan. They came to apprehend the man, not to perform a death-defying balancing act.

Red looked up again and saw her sister closing in on the control box – but then she spotted a couple of broken cables lying across White's path, and Red held her breath. Had her sister seen the obstructions?

"Watch for cables," Red shouted, and then spat out a mouthful of sand. The wind came and went like a passing spirit. When the wind died again, Red repeated her message. White stopped and looked over the framework. "There are cables," Red repeated, frantically pointing up at the hurdle, but now the wind was back and for a moment, the air was filled with harsh, abrasive sand dust.

A sudden movement at the control box had Red turning her head. She squinted her eyes and saw a grey figure move. The man had been waiting all along. He clambered along the arm of the crane, heading towards her sister. White, who was still looking down, and did not know of the impending danger. Red gestured frantically, but it was too late. The man reached for her sister and kicked her hard, knocking one of her legs free.

Red watched as her sister toppled sideways. One of her hands reached for the bar to steady herself... and missed. White toppled forward and Red watched in utter disbelief as her sister disappeared down the mineshaft.

Red let out a huge cry that become lost within the storm. Without concern for her own safety, she descended. Reaching the ground, she went to the edge of the pit and looked over. Red called out her sister's name. The hole, some thirty feet wide, stretched down and vanished into darkness. Red frantically shouted, trying to make her voice rise above that of the noise of the storm. No reply came — at least, none that she could hear.

Old cables ran down into the abyss and she contemplated climbing down, but these wires were metal, and rusted and frayed – her hands would shred in minutes. Then she noted the vulgar looking rocks that jutted out of the tunnel walls. She was sure that her sister could not have survived the fall. Tears filled her eyes and an inner anger grew like a wild fire. A noise alerted her.

She turned, just as the man jumped down from the ladder. He swung his fist, intending to knock her into the hole. Red reacted quickly, dodging his blow and leaping to one side. Her foot landed on uneven rubble, and she tripped and fell. She landed on a heap of tarpaulin and watched as the man ran past her.

Red, filled with anger, got to her feet and scrambled to get moving. White's killer was getting away. Red's mind had space for only one thought, and that was to avenge her sister.

She pulled herself forward, hot tears running freely down her cheeks. Her sister had endured so much, and for what? To die in a pit, her body lying mangled and broken.

The man was quick despite his size. He pulled himself up and over obstacles and flung others out behind him, trying to slow Red down. She dodged around them and gained some ground, but the man had a good head start. And the weather was not helping. At moments, he became just a shade, almost merging with other objects.

Red jumped over the last of the obstacles and forged ahead. The surrounding objects helped to slow the wind and sand and finally, she saw the man passing through the outpost's main gates. He looked back, checking to see her progress. He noticed how she was closing ground, and he put his head down and used every ounce of energy to propel him forward.

Red picked up her speed, calling on an inner strength that she now knew she had. Seeing her sister's abilities had finally made her believe in her own. Her muscles responded and suddenly she was moving quickly as her legs went into overdrive. She powered on through the main gates and saw the man running downhill towards the first of the buildings. She continued on, knowing that if he reached the buildings, she might lose sight of him.

The man ran down the main street. Streams of sand scattered as his feet ran through deep drifts. He was only a short way ahead now. In his panic, he turned off down an alley – and then he stopped. Red, with no time to wonder why he had stopped, ran to him, grabbing hold of his clothing. She cried out with anger, one hand grabbing his cloak, the other clenching into a fist, ready to... then she noticed the bodies.

Some way ahead lay the remains of five or six people. The sand had already half obscured several of the bodies. Darker patches of sand lay about, stained with blood. She recognised one of the security men. His face frozen with fear, his eyes unblinking, his mouth wide and poised to scream.

She looked at the mayhem that littered the narrow street. What happened here, she could not say, but she didn't have time to contemplate the scene. Her anger returned, and she pushed the traveller over – he landed on his back. The man glanced over at the bloodied remains, and a broad smile appeared across his face. Red could not understand why he was smiling, but the sight of that grin filled her full of rage. She dived at him, knocking the air out of his lungs, pelting his face with her fists, trying to wipe away his smug expression.

The man did not defend himself. He still smiling. She made him look up at her.

"You killed my sister, you piece of shit," she said.

The man laughed. "It is too late."

"I don't care if it is too late," Red said, her hands now around his throat. "With the tower down, and this storm in the sky, your message, whatever it was, would have failed – so my sister died for nothing."

The man choked, but he was still laughing. "The message transmitted a while ago. Look," he said, pointing over at the bodies. "We are all dead now. Your sister was just the first."

"I don't understand. Why are we all dead now, and why send a message about my sister?"

The man coughed before replying. "There's a national message. I saw it on my data pad. Syrin has given a reward for information."

"And you responded?" Red said, her inner pain rising in her throat. She shook her head. "But who killed all these people, and why?"

The man laughed as he coughed up blood. "You'll see." He moved his head from side to side. "All you need to know is that I sold the information for my family. It was just about the credits..."

She could not hear any more. An inner anger consumed her until she could no longer see the man. Her hands energised, and she squeezed. Red's mind replayed the image of her helpless sister as she fell into that dark oblivion. She had only just found her, and now she had lost her – what this company wanted with them, she could not speculate, but it seemed that Syrin had dark designs on their future. Red breathed deeply and looked at the man. His face was crimson. She let go of his neck, but it was too late. He was dead.

Red, repulsed by her own actions, wiped her hands down her clothing. Is this what she had become, a cold-blooded killer. She stood up and looked down at the traveller. Sand was already gathering in his sightless eyes. Something distracted Red when a faint sound filtered through the dying wind.

She looked over at a man who was lying face down on the ground. His out-stretched hand was slowly flexing. He was lying in a gigantic pool of blood, with his face turned towards her. Red walked over to him.

Crouching down, she tried to turn the man, but the pain was too much for him. He spoke, his bloodied lips moving to form words.

"Beware," he said. "Something looking... for you."

"What's looking for me?" Red asked.

The man coughed and spluttered. More blood oozed from between his lips. His eyes were rolling back in their sockets. Red shook him. He moaned with pain, and the pain seemed to bring him back.

"What's looking for me?" Red asked again.

The man took a deep breath and said, "Something terrible, something evil," and then his breath escaped his mouth as he died.

She got to her feet. She looked back and thought about the mine. Reason told her to take her ride and start out across the desert. Her feelings, however, told her to be sure that her sister was dead – and she needed to bring back the body. Her heart won the battle.

When Red reached the mine, she was ready in her mind for whatever she would find. The wind had slowed, making her passage easier. Her field of vision became clearer as the sand swirls reduced. As she crossed the field of debris, she happened upon a coil of old rope. The rope was unbelievably heavy. As her hands wrapped around it, her abilities surged, surprising her. Her abilities so far had run to tech items, but now she was feeling things about other items, such as this rope. Now she knew how old the rope was and everything about its synthesis. She was changing at every moment, and here was the proof. Red wasn't sure about these changes and what the result would be. Moving the thought from her mind, she tied one end around the foot of the crane and was about to drop the rest over the side when she detected movement.

Her breath caught in her throat as she listened. Maybe White was alive after all. Then a new sound wafted up, and she shuddered. A rasping laugh came from below. The faint sound of crumbling rock echoed above that of the wind as something clawed its way down. Then, whatever it was, spoke.

"I'm coming to get you, little one," the voice hissed. Red thought about the fallen man's words, *something terrible, something evil*, and shivered.

For a moment, the wind eased further, and she thought she heard the thing land. She waited.

She listened, but then the wind picked up again just as a sound like running met with her ears. A sudden realisation hit her, filling her full of hope. The creature had run off, meaning that it had not found her sister lying at the base of the pit. That surely meant White was still alive.

Red continued to wait, listening. After a moment, she was ready to move again. Surprise might be her only weapon, and she did not want to lose the advantage.

The sounds from below told her that this shaft could not be over sixty or seventy feet deep. She tested the rope again and now felt confident.

Red positioned herself over the edge and walked her feet down. Despite the chase, her body was not that fatigued. Whatever skills she possessed, her body was remembering them, just as her mind remembered fragments of her past.

The descent was relatively easy. A gentle decrease in light became a measure of how far she was travelling.

It was good to be out of the wind, but she could not help wondering what she was about to encounter. First, there was the possibility of finding White's body lying injured in some far corner of the mine. And the strange creature was still roaming about. Her eyes looked at the rough rock. Only something non-human could have navigated the walls without a ladder or line. Was this an off-world creature?

She stopped her descent when the voice of the creature called out. It was faint now, but the echo carried its words back. "Come on out, little one," it said and laughed. The thing was enjoying its game. It did not seem concerned that it was giving away its location. Listening to the hiss in its voice made Red uneasy. Her mind considered all variables, but one thought persisted – Red was on a rescue mission.

Red's shoes suddenly hit the floor. The tunnel continued on, slightly dipping, and at first, she could not work out why she saw so much detail. She looked about, marvelling at how lit the area was. She walked a little way in, went over to the wall, and placed her hand on the cool surface. Her touch and her ability gave her the answer she needed. The rock bed was full of strange minerals, and one of those minerals contained a natural light source. She looked on. The tunnel walls continued. She took a deep breath – time to find White.

Chapter Twenty-Nine

Manark found himself in a small observation room, which had not been here the last time he had frequented the lab. He wondered what other changes Syrin had implemented. A comm desk and three rows of chairs sat before two enormous glass windows, one on either side of another door. Manark went over to one and looked at the lab. The memories came flooding back.

He went to this second door, which had a security pad below a tiny inspection window, and swiped his card. It granted him access. He passed through and looked about.

It was incredible. The details of the room and the faint traces of vat smells were familiar and evoked past feelings. Three long conveyer belts stretched out with various robotic arms on either side. He recalled how the AIs shuffled along on these conveyors as the robot-arms performed their various operations. It had all seemed so harmless to him back then. He had told himself that he was bettering their life, making them complete and helping them to be the best they could. Whatever happened to them after he finished his work must have taken them down a darker path.

He looked at the array of equipment. It was incredible to think that they realised the programmable surgery with only a handful of staff. In the future, fully automated labs would operate with only one scientist needed for analytical duties.

Then he noticed something that was different. Along the way stood several machines – recent additions to the process. He walked along the line and looked at them. They had the same fine injection couplings, but some of them carried cylinders containing unknown liquids. These fluid attachments were add-ons. No wonder the new data readings were so unusual. The three AIs had undergone a complete system upgrade, including several things that went beyond his technical knowledge.

Manark left the machines, moved over to a data panel and turned it on, but nothing happened. Checking the next produced the same response. Looking up, he saw only minimal lighting, meaning that the lab was only on reserve power. Anxiety made his breath catch in his throat. Had he risked all this espionage for nothing?

A relay box caught his eye, farther along the wall. He walked to it, grabbed the red handle, and pulled it to the ON position. The data pads came back to life with a deep hum, and overhead florescent tubes burst into action.

Manark went back to a data pad and typed. It asked him for his pass and he swiped his card. The screen reacted, and he exhaled. He typed again, calling up the Project. He was in, and now he was navigating the system. First, he needed to know if the three AIs were still on the run. Thankfully, the system was such that anything involving the Arin project presented itself within this frame. He searched for updates and found two.

The first update was a copy of his bogus report that Sarak had made him sign. He did not want to think of his signature at the foot of the document, but it reinforced his decision to be here. The second update, however, ignited his interest. The data showed a map. This correspondence mentioned a crash and then a second piece of intel mentioned a small outpost close to Solar 1. The account was enough to convince him it was the last known location of the AIs. He mentally noted the coordinates. It was a simple grid reference because of the area involved, so relatively easy to remember.

Now that he had found a grid point, it was time to shift his attention and find out exactly what Syrin had been doing and why the program had nearly destroyed the very things that it had created.

He gasped several times as he read the new orders and learned about the new programing. Protein replacements, blood Nano implants that carried more oxygen around the organs, and bone infusions. It all pointed to one purpose. The company was making these synthetic humans as strong as possible – building a body that could sustain and endure beyond normal physical capabilities.

The footnotes were almost baleful in their conclusions. One suggested they could replicate the effects on these synthesised life forms in human born subjects. When he looked at the graphs, he had to agree with the findings.

He sat back, mystified. The original intention was to grow something organic that could bridge the gap between humankind and machine. A fundamental factor was the organically grown organs and bone grafting. This new conditioning took the AI production into a different realm altogether. These organic creations did not need super powers, unless Syrin had ulterior motives with a darker intent.

He gazed across at the new injecting machines and wondered. He needed to think about how he could help. Right at this moment, Syrin would have deployed something in its arsenal to intercept the AIs. The two that he could confirm as still living probably had a whole heap of trouble heading their way.

He could take one of the company air-cars. The runaways needed to learn what they were and how they could overturn the company – but right now they needed more than words. They needed an aid.

He looked again at the silent machines.

Their arms, with their medically precise implements, stood poised, ready to perform tasks at the hit of a button. Manark took a deep breath. Could it work? he wondered. There was no guarantee he would survive the installation. According to what he had just gleaned, the body boost was quick. However, it was AI collated data and not human. All ideas of what it would do to a human born subject were pure speculation.

He tapped his key pad furiously. He called up programing and then installations. It was all there, the schematics, the belt diagnostics and operating starts. These extra alterations would only take up to ten brief minutes. He looked at the conveyor belt and knew that the program would oversee the work. All he had to do was hit a couple of keys.

Manark slapped his chest with his hands and took three deep breaths. He stood up and stripped down to his underwear. Then he returned to the keyboard and accessed the new phase additions. The program activated. Three machines came into life. The belt moved. The track would not stop until its sensors registered a host.

A large cabinet stood against the wall and he went to it. The cabinet had a code sensor-lock. He used his elbow to smash the thin glass. Then he reached inside and forced the mechanism.

The cabinet was untouched, with all the swabs and sterilisers still in place. He opened the door and grabbed hold of an inoculator. Then he grabbed a bottle of anesthetising solution and applied it to an injection gun. He shot the solution into his arm and then the other arm – double the usual dosage – he did the same to his chest area. He repeated the process for his lower body. Manark did not know how much pain he could take, or what reactions the advancements would cause, and he hoped he had sedated his body accordingly.

He walked over to the conveyor belt and looked along the line at the waiting machines. This was it. He felt a surge of coldness coursing through his body. He pinched his arm and felt nothing. Then a noise had him turning his head. Back at the start of the room, people were entering the observation room.

Manark raced towards the viewing windows. He had to stop them before they entered, and he had to be quick. Once the numbing effect fully took hold of his limbs, he would not be able to move. He had maybe minutes before these effects took hold.

More people entered the demonstration area. They parted when security appeared. He could see them fumbling to find their override passkey. He felt his body getting cooler. If he froze before he got himself back to the conveyor belts, he would just fall to the floor and lie there, helpless. He reached the observation windows and stopped.

Manark grabbed a fire-tank from its housing and carried it over to the door swipe. He brought the tank down on the panel twice and then watched as sparks erupted like a fountain of light. Several sparks hit his body, but he felt nothing. People, some of them wearing lab coats, scattered when he slammed the tank against the door. The security finally produced their passkey.

The guard looked at Manark, and they swapped glances. Manark could not see what security was doing, because the door area only had a small face panel. The guard fumbled about for a moment, then stopped.

Manark nodded his head, which made the guard mad with rage. He was shouting something, but the soundproofing muffled his words. He pounded the glass with his fist, but Manark knew his actions were futile. The inspection windows and the door were solid. Unless the guards got hold of a cutting tool, they would not gain access.

The guard was still silently beating the door as Manark ambled away. It was time. The lab ran on its own power source in case of failure, so Syrin could not stop the operation by shutting down the facility. As he walked back, he noted how he could no longer feel the floor beneath his feet. He reached for the moving belt.

He looked over his shoulder and saw the watching crowd part. Sarak appeared at the glass and gazed at him. Her face moved closer to the large inspection panel – her goggles touched the glass, and she considered him. She did not allow herself to react, because that would only highlight how powerless she was at that moment. Her eyes were unblinking as she studied him.

Manark gave her a small salute. Then he threw himself onto the conveyor belt and let it carry him forward. He looked up at the bright lights and then at the overhanging machines that came into view.

He tried to control his breathing. It was strange that he, a scientist, should be the first human born test subject. The belt stopped. He was now in place. It was time to discover what all the data had shown. He tried to lift his arm, but his muscles were unresponsive. The last command he had given the computer was to administer a stimulant to reawaken his body once the surgery was over. The machine hummed gently and the arm of the robot moved across his chest – Manark closed his eyes.

Chapter Thirty

After the heat of the surface, the seam of the mine felt cool. The dense rock gave off a slight sulphurous odour. Red marvelled at how much she could see, despite the gloom. Then she remembered the nightstick. She checked her pocket, feeling for the item. What she found was her hand-cannon. She cursed the fact that she had forgotten about it after buying it from the vendor in Solar 3. She had wasted her time chasing the travelling man when all she had to do was shoot him down. Red checked her other pocket and discovered that the night-stick was missing. She hoped that the light producing mineral illuminated the rest of the mine.

The floor dipped downward. Red continually looked about for any sign of her sister, or the creature, but saw nothing. She reached a new section and noticed tiny steps carved into the rock. To her side, at waist height, ran a hover rail. The magnetised carriages were long gone, but further along lay a platform. The workers had scattered discarded supplies about the dusty surface, as if they had left in a hurry.

Red looked about. Had her sister really come this way? If she had, it went some way to proving that her injuries were not major. She looked about – the mine felt oppressive. What had happened to the beast she wondered? Was he hiding, or had he found her sister and carried her off?

Red came alongside a loader. It sat there, a thin coating of glowing material still gracing its bed. It was brighter here, and she looked about for any trace of footprints, but found none. Beside the loader stood a mound of boxes. She brushed debris from their lids and opened them. The first box was empty, but the second had one remaining item lying in its corner.

The charge was no bigger than her fist. Even as she picked it up, her ability tingled into life, releasing the object's secrets. A Sabion charge, no longer recognised by safety control as a usable piece of equipment. Still, a valuable find, she thought to herself, especially as a throwing weapon. The blast would take out a small wall... or a foe.

She pushed the item deep into her cloak pocket and continued, feeling a little more secure.

The ground levelled out again and opened into a large area. The mine had installed several huts down here. She walked forward, her body bent into a protective stoop. She carefully brought out her hand cannon and held it out before her. Her ability sensed that the device was now down to a quarter power. She hoped it was enough.

The door of the first cabin was open. She stepped inside and recoiled at the dank, sulphurous stench. The room did not need strong lighting for her to tell that this was a toilet. She quickly exited.

The second hut seemed to be some kind of rest area. Discarded seats and tables lay bare and forgotten. Charts hung on the wall, and over the way, ran a large window. A box of crystal fragments lay on a table, giving off light. She picked up one of the larger fragments. It weighed next to nothing. It radiated a sufficient amount of light, so Red put the item into her pocket.

She exited the cabin and stopped. She heard shuffling. The temptation to call out White's name was strong, but she did not know if it was her sister or her unwanted guest. Maybe it was neither, she told herself. Maybe the old mine was relaxing and what she was hearing was the fall of tiny rocks.

Hearing no other sounds, Red continued. She still had her cannon held out before her. Despite the half-light, her eyes were now adapting well. A scattering of rock-waste lay on the ground, and a discarded boot in one corner. Small pools of water had collected, despite the desert lying above.

The area ahead widened further and now the tunnel split into two and still her sister remained elusive. Why had White gone so deep into the tunnel? Maybe she was looking for another way out, she reasoned. The pit shaft was unclimbable without equipment. Red cursed the fact that she had run away, chasing the traveller. She could have dropped her sister a line and that would have been an end to it. However, she was forgetting one bizarre fact. She could still picture her sister falling down into the dark mine. How had she survived such a fall? Red wiped the puzzle from her mind. What she realised was that the creature had appeared and White had moved deeper into the mine to escape discovery.

Looking about, she considered her options. The monorail continued down the left-hand side, but the other tunnel had a clear walkway.

She was still contemplating her options when something moved. The shape shuffled forward and Red felt her heart quicken.

"White," she whispered, looking at the approaching figure. Then, as the person left the shadows, they seemed to grow. Red needed to be certain that this was the creature and not the man from the outpost.

She knelt down, took out her crystal, and threw it over to where the person stood. Red gasped as she gazed upon the creature that the dying man had described.

The lizard-like animal stopped and looked down at the crystal and then back at Red. Two yellow eyes with black, narrow pupils considered her. Then the thing chuckled. The last of its laugh came out as a quick hiss.

"Don't come near me," Red said.

The thing looked about as if it had all the time in the world. Evidently, it did not consider her much of a threat.

The Reptile man turned to face her again and its mouth opened, displaying rows of needle-like teeth.

"You are easy prey."

Red was not about to debate the creature's words as she pulled out her cannon and fired. A sound-blast ripped through the air and hit the animal squarely in the chest. The figure flew back twelve or more feet before landing on its back.

Standing in an open area was not good, she decided. With the cannon still out before her, she turned and ran over to a hut. The two cabins lay very close together, with only the smallest of margins between them both. The creature would have no option but to squeeze in between if it wanted her. Maybe then she would have it at a disadvantage. The beast would be vulnerable. She could shoot at its face and it would be powerless to dodge the blow.

She slid between the two buildings and waited. A shuffling sound came her way. Red wondered how wounded the creature was.

More foot falls and Red tensed, holding the cannon out before her. The thing stopped. It was close enough for Red to hear it sniffing the air.

An almighty grating sound confused Red at first, but then she saw how the wall of the cabin was sliding away from her. It showed just how much power the creature possessed.

Red looked over her shoulder for a way out before she became exposed. Behind her, at the other end of the cabins, stood a hard wall – and indeed, a dead end. There was only one way out, and that was forward. Well done, she mentally said. You have backed yourself into a corner and now it has you.

The animal stepped out into the space that it had created. As soon as it came into view, Red let go another sonic boom.

The thing before her flew backwards as the sound-waves hit home. It slammed against the floor, air spilling from its mouth in a rasping hiss. Another sound came from its long snout, and at first Red thought it a cry of pain. It was not. It was a deep chuckle. The thing on the ground was testing both her and her weapon, and it seemed mildly amused by both.

Red watched the lizard rise into a standing position. Its breast plate had vanished, destroyed by the blast, leaving fragments littering the floor. The beast touched its face with one long, bony finger. The scales on one side of its jaw were bleeding. It looked at the secretion, licked its finger, and laughed again. Its eyes narrowed when they looked back at Red. Its smile vanished.

Her gun was losing power with each blast. She had ten, maybe twelve shots left before the chamber reached empty. She let go another sonic blast as the creature was staring at her.

The blast flung the lizard-man backward, but this time the thing kept its balance. The animal's arms flexed and its bare, bootless feet scored the rock with its hard, talon-like claws.

Red moved herself back as far as she could. The huts now lay in a v shape. The rock face came up behind her. She imagined the beast suddenly charging her, but it disappeared from view. She stood watching. Was this a trick – should she make a run for it? Then the wall of the hut was moving in on her and she realised what was happening. The creature was now pushing the huts together.

The huts moved quickly. She placed her hands on the advancing panel and realised that she did not have enough time to run the length of the building before the two sides met. Only one option remained. She squatted down and slipped herself under the advancing hut. Thankfully, the cabins stood on sturdy legs, providing a foot of space beneath.

The buildings above slammed together, displacing dirt and dust. Red had only just made it in time. The misty air filled her nostrils and blinded her eyes as she fumbled to turn her body. Her weapon slipped from her fingers and dropped to the floor. Her hands slid across the rough ground, searching for her cannon. She coughed several times and wiped grime from her eyes. Her hand moved, searching, feeling nothing but soil and grit. Then she stopped. Her pulse throbbed in her neck. She watched as the beast walked along the side of the hut. Then it was down on one knee, bending, its hand coming into the space to search.

Red took a moment to feel for the elusive gun. The beast reached further and Red had to move back.

Panic surged within her – she was weapon-less. All she could do now was out manoeuvre the creature.

The beast's large hand came dangerously close. Red pushed herself towards the outer edge of the cabin, frantically trying to get away from the reaching claws. She was nearly out the other side when the beast lashed out and caught hold of her trailing robe. Red felt her body slide as the animal pulled her back. She kicked out, her boots slipping on the debris. Then Red rolled onto her side, trying to free herself from the grip. She tried to discard her clothing, but the crawl space was too restricting.

The beast brought its head down to the floor, gazing at her with its yellow eyes. It opened its long mouth and Red saw the waiting teeth. She neared the biting mouth, her feet desperately trying to escape its bite.

Taking a deep breath, Red let her mind fight away her panic and think towards a solution. Most creature's heads had two weaknesses; one being the eyes, and the other being the tip of the nose. Red pulled her leg back and waited for the thing to strike. Just as the gaping jaw came her way once more, a boot came down on the creature's outstretched neck, pinning it flat against the rock bed with a slam. The lizard thing's eyes went wide, and the beast cried out. Red gazed at the boot and realised that it was White.

The lizard man quickly forgot about Red and released its hold on her as it tried to protect itself from the attack.

Red moved herself away and out from under the building, feeling a familiar object brush her hand as she moved. Grasping the cannon, she turned the gun on the reptile, then lined up the sights with the beast's face, which was still under the hut. She shouted out to warn White. The beast, seeing the cannon aiming toward its head, used every ounce of energy to move away. The sonic blast wormed out and hit the side of the creature's face, sending it back. As the beast rolled along the ground, one of its large outstretched arm slammed against White's legs, spinning her in the air.

Red looked away, frantically pushing herself out from the under the building. As she squeezed out, she noticed a long bloodied gash on her arm, but ignored the injury. Picking herself up, she ran along the side of the hut and then around the front, racing past the open doorway.

Her feet slapped against the hard floor as she rounded the corner – then she froze. The beast was already on its feet. Her sister was now lying a short distance away, her mouth bloodied from landing on a jutting rock, her expression dazed.

Red moved forward, but the thing was quick. The creature turned its wounded head. It had lost an eye.

Opening its snout, it hissed violently and came running towards her. She aimed the cannon, but not in time as the beast reached her, slapping its huge hands against her chest.

Air escaped her lungs as she flew backwards. She landed in a heap, her head slapping hard against the floor. Red felt a wetness seeping into her clothing, and she did not know if it was blood or wet earth. Pain coursed through her body as she lifted her arm to fire. A blast shot forward but missed its mark and slammed into a far wall, sending splinters of rock in every direction. For a moment, the sound echoed around the chamber, but already it was fading into nothing. Then the beast gave a long, rasping cry and started forward.

Red lifted her cannon again. She pulled the trigger and nothing happened. She repeated the operation a second time with the same results. Her senses told her that the gun had enough fluid for several more blasts. Then she refocussed her abilities, searching the item before discovering that her gun's mechanism had jammed.

The beast slowly advanced. One of its legs was not responding. Blood ran freely down its face and neck. The wound on its chest looked deep. It seemed to savour the fact that Red was now powerless. Movement caught her attention. She looked beyond the beast and saw her sister trying to rise. Then she remembered something.

She reached deep into her pocket and found the small explosive grenade. Pressing a switch with her index finger, she armed the device. Red bided her time, waiting for the creature to come closer. The reptile was taking its time, enjoying the moment. It laughed and hissed, spitting blood as it shuffled forward, trailing its injured leg.

Red was panting. This was it. The beast was close enough now. Any closer and the blast might injure her as well. She pulled her hand from under her cloak. As she lifted her hand up, the reptile spied on what she was holding and faltered. It was too late. Red threw the device. The creature flew back again as the grenade met with its body and exploded. The beast landed and lay still, its bulk crumpled and beaten. Wounds across its torso welled with blood. Its head lay unmoving, its great jaws gaping, its tongue lolling to one side as bloody saliva dribbled out and ran onto the ground.

Red rested her head back and panted for breath, blinking her eyes several times. Then she turned her head. White was standing with her hands placed on both knees as she collected herself.

The pain in Red's body surged for a moment before stabilising. A feeling activated deep within her as whatever abilities she possessed surged into life. An inner warmth spread from limb to limb. She lay still and controlled her breathing. She waited for the warmth to reach her chest.

An inner sense made Red lift her head. A feeling of terror clenched her throat tight as she watched the reptile creature sit back up. It looked straight at her. For a moment, she could not breathe or speak, her throat paralysed with fear. She looked over at her sister and realise that she had her back to the animal and could not see the foe rising. Red tried to lift herself, but her chest complained.

The beast quietly got to its feet. White was the nearest, and it needed to gain an advantage. Equalling the numbers would do that. The reptilian thing seemed to draw the last of its energy. It bared its teeth. Clearly, it wanted to finish what it had started and no amount of injury was going to stand in its way.

Red found her voice and shouted out, using every ounce of breath – but the beast was already lunging.

Chapter Thirty-One

D espite the influx of nerve numbing injections, Manark had his teeth clenched against the pain. The robot above him clicked and bleeped as it went about its various programs. Pistons flexed as delicate implements pierced his soft flesh. Another arm came around carrying a long injection, while another waited with a scalpel. A third stood poised with a surgical stapler.

The pain was near unbearable. He wished he had a further dose of numbing serum. He knew that the three original test subjects would have had none. The pain they must have endured was unfathomable.

After this section of surgery had finished, the conveyor belt suddenly jolted and Manark moved forward to the fourth and final robotic arm. Then he heard an extra noise and before the machine could start, he lifted his head and looked back down the line.

He could still see many faces watching him like a peepshow crowd. Some were gazing at him while others watched the security door. That was when Manark realised the cause of this unfamiliar noise. Sparks were flying in every direction as security used their cutting equipment.

The last machine on the belt suddenly activated, and it set about its task. Manark looked down. The machine was finishing what other machines had done to his lower limbs. His legs had fared better in the pain stakes, but he knew that this would soon change.

He could move about more now that the machine was working on his legs. He looked back at the inspection room and noticed how a young female operative moved out of the way. Then Sarak's gaunt face appeared at the glass.

He could not quite make out her eyes from this distance, but he felt their gaze. She looked over at the security door and so did Manark. A neat line appeared around the lock. Sarak turned her face back towards him and nodded, as if quietly optimistic that she would win the day. This was good, Manark thought. Most histories' failures were born out of over confidence. Still, he watched the line being cut around the lock and hoped that the robot conducting this last piece of surgery was quicker than the cutting equipment.

He glanced at his lower limbs and found that the droid had finished with his left leg. A stapler arm was busy sealing the deep tissue. Then the bot continued, puncturing the flesh in order to attach a deeper membrane. Then it became busy injecting the specialised fluid. The numbness was slowly wearing off and his legs burned. Bruising quickly spread across his upper thighs, but as quickly as the colouring appeared, the influx of super solution cleared away the pigmentation. His bodily alterations were already performing miracles. Across the lab, the cutting tool continued to inch its way around the lock.

Manark flexed his arms, testing them. They still felt a little inactive, but the pain was already receding, which he found remarkable. What he felt was not unlike sunburn. He tensed a fist and marvelled at the definition of his forearm. He felt youth and vitality, as if time had reversed. Part of him wanted the guards to gain entrance so he could assert his newfound powers and see just what he could do.

When he relaxed his fists, he noticed how his forearms reduced back to their original size. So now, he could enhance his muscles as needed. It was incredible.

The bot beside his legs gave a final injection, clicked and swung away. Then it turned off and stood idle.

Manark swung his legs off the belt and looked back toward the entrance.

They had nearly broken the lock. He saw Sarak turn her head and shout something at the maintenance men. When she returned her gaze to the glass, her cool demeanour had vanished. She leaned forward. Her goggles and her forehead slapped against the pane, as if she wanted to break it with her pressure.

Taking a deep breath, Manark dropped off the conveyor belt... and collapsed on the floor. His legs were unresponsive. He panicked. Frantically, he massaged his upper and lower legs. He looked back and saw the cutting tool move inch by inch. Five more inches and the locking plate would give.

He grabbed the conveyor belt, and he heaved himself up, feeling his new muscle density expand and retract in the same motion. Then, on shaking legs, he willed himself to walk. His lower limbs were growing in strength with every step, but he was still plodding. The lock was now three inches away from giving. Sarak was screaming obscenities at the security. He could not hear her, but he could see her thin mouth slapping away.

He moved himself down the aisle, grabbing on to whatever he found. It was darker here. Manark knew the emergency tunnel door lay somewhere near the back and hoped that it was visible.

Pushing himself forward, he passed several booths, all of which contained vast stocks of fluids. For a moment, he contemplated trying to ignite them, but he did not know how flammable they were.

There it was. He spotted the door. It was just like any other fire door, but it had some kind of resin block running across as a deterrent.

He reached the exit door as they broke through the locking mechanism at the other end of the lab. Manark looked back as the metal plate landed with a clatter. The door flew open and six guards spilled into the lab.

Manark placed his hands on the exit door and pushed. It held fast. Then he looked at the locking pin and he applied pressure to that area. He heard the bar creak and then he applied more pressure. His arms were filling with the new fluid and relaying power to his muscles. The long pin gave and fell to the floor. He opened the doors and entered the cool air of the corridor.

The tunnel in front of him lay mostly in darkness, save for the green, glowing health and safety lights.

Manark looked back. The guards were half way down the room. He closed the emergency doors behind him.

A large metal maintenance locker stood near. He grabbed hold of the sides, ripped it from its support bracket, and sent it toppling across the double doors just as the guards came beating at the exit.

Manark stepped back when he heard them try to push the doors open – the locker held. Sensing that the obstacle would not hold for long, he turned and ran down the tunnel.

His legs had recovered and felt full of energy, an energy that he had never known, not even as a child. He felt like a superman. His lower limbs propelled him down the corridor at a dizzying speed.

He reached an adjoining section, looked both ways, and read a sign on the wall. Hover Park C was on the south side of the building. He had never been there, but at least he would be out of the principal building. The other indicator read Recessions. He did not know what this was and did not want to take a chance.

As he travelled, he marvelled at his new abilities. He felt like a speeding tank. Right at that moment, Sarak was probably dialling the main frame and asking where the tunnel led. All the upper executives had their own escape elevators, should a rebel attack happen. Sarak would not know about these other escape corridors. Reason told him she would amass a large security team, but that team would not have the time for a briefing.

An exit appeared, and he charged towards it, not knowing what was on the other side. The swinging door might take out a couple of guards if they were waiting on the other side.

The doors broke open. One came off its hinge. Manark smacked into a stationary hover car and dented the side panel. He looked around, but Park C was just a mass of vehicles with no sign of waiting security.

He checked his body for injuries. Just one scratch, which was self-healing even as he watched. Then he looked at the damage to the hover car and shook his head in disbelief.

A shouting voice had him turning. Three guards came running from the other end of the bay. One of them was pulling out a blaster, another was calling into his portable comm device, and the third guard put his head down, pumping his limbs as fast as he could.

The line of cars was just a blur as Manark ran. He knew that the guard with the gun would not fire unless they were in proximity – too many vehicles containing explosive fluids. As he ran, Manark scanned each vehicle for a Syrin logo. The corporation's courtesy cars were primed, ready for visitors to use. Speeding past a silver car, he spotted something and stopped. Backing up, he read the tell-tale logo. He had found what he needed.

He reached for the door, but a sudden movement made him turn.

A beefy guard slammed into him, knocking Manark off his feet. With surprising agility, Manark untangled himself from the guard's grip and stood up.

The guard staggered back and readied himself for a further assault. He suddenly charged forward, intending to put Manark back on the ground. This time, Manark was ready, and his balance was better. The guard's hands hit Manark's chest and Manark heard the man's wrists snap back. The guard cried out and fell to the ground, writhing in pain.

"Occupational hazard," Manark said to the fallen guard as he pulled open the door to the car.

The plush interior greeted his body, and he realised he was still wearing nothing but his underwear. He pressed the access card, which he had found suspended from a switch near the control panel, and the engine ignited.

A thump had Manark turning. The other two guards had reached the car and were thumping on the glass. One of them took out a small blaster and fired at the window, intending to shoot right through the panel and take him out. The blast ricocheted off in several directions. One spark of light hit the guard, who quickly covered his stinging face.

Rolling his eyes, Manark turned his attention back to the control panel. The stupidity of the guard made him shake his head – all Syrin vehicles were mob-proof. And the guard could have taken himself and everybody else with him, if his ricocheting bullet had hit a fuel area.

It was a fully automated vehicle. Manark scrolled down and found a list of destination sectors. He chose one at random. As long as he left the quadrant and put some distance between him and the corporation, all would be well. He could then reprogram new coordinates.

Engines started. Steaming vapours hissed as the car levitated. Then he was travelling forward. He sailed past the neat rows of hover cars and left the exit. The car automatically paused for traffic and then rose upwards and was soon just another silver box flying across the city.

Flexing his hands to feel the underlining power, he exhaled and then sat back in his seat. He closed his eyes and sighed. A sudden sensation began in his mind, and he panicked. He tried to fight the pulsing, but the feeling grew inside him, filling his head, consuming him. Had he put himself through all that pain for it to backfire at the last moment? But then a voice spoke to him, deep within his mind, telling him not to fight the feelings and the connection.

Manark gasped. "Blue, is that you?"

"I can only speak for a moment," the voice said, and echoed and shifted with each word so that it became many voices. "You don't yet possess a genuine connection but that will change." The voice drifted for a moment, and just when Manark thought it wouldn't continue, he heard the voice speak again. "The girls are still alive, and as far as I can sense, they are well and together."

Again, Manark sighed, his whole body relaxing. "Thank you," he said, but the voice, which he believed to be Blue, spoke again.

"Go towards Solar 1. Search that region."

"That's an awfully sizeable area to search?" he replied.

"You will know when you are there. For now, do not worry. I must go."

Manark responded but got no answer. He waited and realised that the link had closed. Answers. It was all about answers. There seemed no end to it at all. The more you knew, the greater the amount of questions that presented themselves. Did he now possess some kind of telepathic ability? He let the question fade as he thought about the advice. Do not worry. That was all he could do at that moment. He consoled himself with the knowledge of knowing the girls were safe and together. This gave him strength and purpose. And now he had a rough idea of which sector on this great planet they were inhabiting. He turned his head and looked out the window.

Manark watched as the Syrin tower became lost in the vast array of city buildings. He was free, free to find the three AIs. He just hoped that time was on his side. Only then, seeing the many monolithic buildings speed past, did he really relax? He allowed himself a moment of jubilation. Manark pictured Sarak's face, and he laughed. He laughed for quite a while.

Chapter Thirty-Two

A scream broke free from Red's mouth. It sounded strange as it ricocheted off the walls. The beast was pumping its body forward as best it could. With one leg floundering, it still built speed. She didn't want to look as it reached her sister... and ran on past.

She gasped. The creature was ignoring her sister. Then Red realised what was happening. The lizard man knew he had been beaten – trying to take them both out was not an option. She guessed her grenade had turned the tide and now the beast was using what energy it had left to get even. And she was a sitting target because her body was still healing.

The Reptilian man advanced. His injuries were substantial, but his desire to kill was greater. Red could feel something happening within her body. A surge built within her. It ran through her veins and her muscles – even her skeleton was filling with a renewed sense of strength. Her body was responding well, but time had run out. The beast was nearly upon her.

She lifted her arms to block herself as the creature lurched forward with its mighty claws flexing. The beast's face was a bloodied mess, its snarling mouth gaping and determined. Red aimed her cannon again and prayed that she had one last shot. She pulled the trigger, closed her eyes and hoped. A familiar empty click sounded. The cannon was useless, so she dropped it... and waited.

The beast's cry made Red flinch – but nothing happened. She opened her eyes and saw her sister pulling the thing away. White pulled the lizard off its feet. It landed with a slap and lay twitching, but still the creature had a little life left.

The beast lifted its head and tried to move. White clenched her hand into a fist, her bicep filling with blood, building beyond what was normal. She quickly brought her fist down, serving a powerful blow to the animal's chest. The foe let out a deathly cry and then lay still. Escaping breath was the creature's last hiss. Finally, the beast was no more.

Red released a loud cry. She let her head fall back. Hot tears ran down her cheeks. She breathed deeply.

Her rejuvenation had reached her mid-section now, and soon her body's self-healing process would be complete. Tired and strained muscles knitted back into place, accompanied by an escalating soothing sensation. Now her hands grew warm and the many scars and cuts on her flesh were smoothing out, as if they were never there.

Red saw White lean over her.

"Lie still and let yourself heal."

"You have that ability as well, don't you?" Red asked.

White nodded her head. "When I fell down the shaft, I thought I was going to die. I lay at the bottom, paralysed – but something stirred deep inside me. I could feel my body fixing itself. It had not fully finished when I heard something moving about at the top of the pit. Then I saw something look over. I knew it wasn't you."

Red nodded her head. Now the healing process was coursing through her upper chest and shoulders. Soon she would feel complete again, with no physical signs of injury.

"I think my healing powers are quicker than yours," White said.

"Alright, no need to brag," Red joked, her tears still rolling down the cheeks of her face. She put out a hand for her sister to pull her up.

Red turned and looked over at the body of the creature. She studied it – the massive torso, the long, muscular arms and hard bony snout. She removed her gaze – they had been so lucky. White leaned in and they embraced.

What seemed like a bolt of electricity suddenly jolted their bodies? A collective image formed in their minds – it was a picture of a person. The image was vague and out of focus. The shape kept shifting in and out. Something told them that the person was trying to communicate with them.

Red was no longer aware of her sister. The image of a young man's face had formed to fill her vision. She did not feel afraid. All she felt was warmth and light. This light was soothing and strangely full of promise. The person looked so serene as his features came into focus. The face was smooth and uncomplicated. Two eyes, full of wisdom, gazed at them. Those delicate features had the same characteristics as herself and White.

"Blue, is that you?" Red heard her sister ask.

"You are so far away," they heard him respond. "You must journey to me."

His voice, which sounded so strong, was now growing faint.

"Where are you?" Red asked.

"Look to the city. Search Trillian," And then, as quickly as it had come, the connection broke. His voice echoed into nothing. The wonderful warming light had also gone, leaving only the dank smelling of mine, with its rough, jagged walls.

Red broke her embrace. "Did you feel that? Did you hear his words?"

White was nodding her head. "That was our brother. He was in the crash too – I know that now."

"Why did he leave us?" Red asked, her breath catching in her throat.

White shook her head. "He must have had a reason. He acted for the better... he loves us."

Red nodded her head. It was true. She felt his love shining through the message. She could not yet understand why he had left them, but she instinctively knew she must trust his reasoning. Until he stood before them, she had to be content with this, and try not to ponder his actions.

White took one last look at the body of the creature and said that it was time to leave. They walked back along the glistening corridor of rock. The ground rose once more, and they eventually reached the shaft entrance.

The rope was still hanging. A fierce sun shone down from above, illuminating their way. It was a new day in the Solar lands. They could already tell that the dawn sand storm had passed, and when they exited, a fierce heat greeted them.

"I thought the fall had killed you," Red admitted as she pulled her sister up to the surface.

White shook her head. "The pain was awful. I really thought my time had come. Where were you?"

Red explained about the man from the crane – how she chased him down to the town and how she had found the bloodied remains of several people, including the security guard.

"Did you kill the traveller?" White asked.

Red averted her eyes for a moment and nodded her head to say yes.

White lifted her sister's chin, so that she was looking at her again. "You came back for me. I will never forget that," Then her face looked grave. "I am so glad I went deeper into the mine. If I had waited, I could not have killed it by myself, especially with my injuries. You distracted the creature long enough for me to regenerate."

Red looked back down into the hole. The creature was down there, surrounded by rock – the mine was now its grave.

"It must have been Syrin that sent that creature to hunt us," White said, breaking Red's thoughts.

Red looked her sister in the eye. "I know it was. They received information about our location."

White stared back, her brow furrowed. "How do you know that?"

"Our traveller told me, down in the town. He told me what Syrin had sent before he... before he died."

White continued to stare at her as she processing the information. "And he said that? He told you he had informed Syrin. Why would he do that?"

Red relayed what the traveller had said, especially about Syrin calling for information.

"But he didn't say why they are seeking us?" White questioned.

"All he wanted was the money," Red replied.

Remembering that they still had the town to navigate, Red put her hands upon her sister's shoulders. "We need to be cautious as we leave. Now that the sand storm had ended, the people might find the bodies and think we did it. In fact, I *know* they will think we killed them – after all, they were probably doing their rounds, checking that we left like we said we would."

Red noted the look of trepidation on her sister's face. White shook her head and sighed. Red gave her a reassuring squeeze of her hand.

They travelled quickly, the harsh sunlight making their passage much easier. Obstacles were easy to spot, and soon they had left the mine area.

They reached the first of the outpost buildings and peered around the corner. Red was right. About fifty people had gathered. Some of them were standing about as a team gathered up the carnage.

Red knew that her sister was more the muscle, and herself, more the brains. Their rides were waiting outside the drinking establishment, but that was far too visible. If they travelled down the back of the buildings, however, they could avoid the major stretch and quickly gather their animals and leave. She whispered the plan to her sister, and she nodded her head in agreement.

They travelled silently along the back of the buildings, dodging lit windows and open passages. White even found some discarded food for their animals. Obstacles made what should have been a brief journey last longer than expected, but soon they emerged right beside their rides.

Their animals looked up as they quickly unshackled them. Red glanced down the road at the busy crowd. Turning their animals, they silently slipped away, back onto the trail that had led them here.

"Where are we going now?" White asked.

"We need to get to Solar One and then buy our way to Trillian."

She noted how her sister's face brightened. "You mean to find our brother?"

Red nodded her head. "That's the plan."

White reached across and grabbed her sister's hand. "I'm so glad we're together."

Red nodded in agreement. However, her mind quickly turned to other thoughts. They were a dirty secret that a corporation wanted quashing. She could now picture a room. This Syrin had done despicable things to them. An intuition told her they were part of some experiment. She recalled a tank with various apparatus. Had they escaped this experiment? Had they stolen a ship to get away? Was this the reason that people were after them? She looked over at White. She was quite innocent, really. However, her abilities were already proving how special they were. Red could already feel the changes deep within herself, too, which slightly frightened her.

So much had happened to them in such a brief span of time. Luck had brought them together, but she knew they must work hard if they wanted to escape their pursuers – and what kind of person was this elusive brother who had contacted them? He said he was in the city. Had the corporation recaptured him, and if not, why had he returned to Trillian? What was his purpose? The more they found answers, the less that things made sense. Glancing across at her sister again made her heart feel good and full – she was so glad they were together. Red made a promise to herself that on no account would she lose her again.

The desert stretched out before them. The gentle rocking of the beast beneath soothed her, and soon she was drifting into a light sleep. Another day, Red thought. They had survived, and that must mean something. She let fatigue claim her, sending her into fitful dreams where things appeared in her mind. Some brought warmth, and some made no sense at all.

ΔBOUT THE ΔUTHOR

Michael Britten graduated from Wolverhampton University with a BA (hons) in Illustration. The cover illustration is one of his designs. Michael spends his free time playing guitar and riding his motorcycle. Rogue Red is his first published book in The Arin Trilogy.

Printed in Great Britain
by Amazon